In the tapestry of history woven under the imposing shadow of the British Raj in India, a colourful yet underrepresented thread belongs to a remarkable group of sailors, known as the *"lascars"*. This distinct cadre of maritime workers emerged prominently during the operational years of the British East India Company, playing a pivotal role in bridging the vast expanses of ocean between the British Empire and its prized colonial possession, India.

Rooted deeply in the territories of British India, lascars were an amalgamation of diverse ethnic and religious backgrounds, primarily consisting of Indian sailors. Despite being considered British subjects, their professional lives were markedly overshadowed by glaring disparities. Governed by the distinctly tailored Asiatic or Lascar Articles, their contractual terms significantly deviated from those of their British counterparts. This bespoke set of regulations permitted a system that was conspicuous for its inequitable compensation structures and differential treatment methods. Lascars found themselves grappling with diminished wages, scant dietary allocations, and cramped living conditions aboard the vessels they served.

The recruitment landscape for lascars were meticulously mapped around the British East India Company's industrial bastions located across various Indian locales such as Bengal, Assam, and Gujarat. Recruitment strategies were chiefly orchestrated by pivotal figures known as *"Ghat Sarhangs"* and their aides, the *"Tindals."* These individuals wielded substantial authority and responsibilities, acting as indispensable linchpins in the maritime operational machinery. They functioned as crucial conduits of communication and coordination, linking the lascars with their White superiors and mitigating linguistic and cultural barriers.

The influence of Ghat Sarhangs and Tindals was not merely confined to the spheres of recruitment and translation. Their roles were imbued with an expansive range of functionalities, extending into the realms of operational management and disciplinary administration aboard the ships. They were instrumental in managing a plethora of shipboard activities, ensuring the smooth navigation of daily routines and exerting authoritative control reflective of the hierarchical paradigms prevalent in the maritime dominions of the era.

Upon arrival on Britannia's harsh shores, lascars were often left adrift in a tempest of neglect and desolation. The labyrinthine streets became the theatre of their desolation, where the dance of survival unfolded in the freezing winds and amongst the shadows of indifference. There, a tapestry of multiracial communities began to weave stories of struggle and existence amidst the harsh symphony of adversity. So, in the gloom of foreign skies and in the suffocating embrace of merciless seas, the saga of the lascars unfurled—a tale woven with threads of survival and struggle, love and loss, dreams haunted by the spectre of cruel fates, and hopes flickering in the relentless storms of destiny.

Endeavouring across vast oceans and turbulent seas, the lascars cast a formidable legacy that resonated across the corridors of maritime history up until the 1960s. Their journeys, imbued with tales of courage, perseverance, and hardship, stand as a testament to the robust contributions made towards the maritime enterprises of the British Empire, despite the shadows of inequity and hardship that loomed over their professional odysseys.

PROLOGUE

In the tumultuous tides of 1856, an epic saga unfolded on the vast, thunderous seas and in the murky, cobbled streets of Britannia—a tale woven in the dark, merciless looms of the East India Company. From the enigmatic shores of India, a wave of lascars, and tireless workers were summoned, pulled from the warm embrace of their native soil and thrust into the bone-chilling winds of an indifferent land and the scorching fires of steam-powered monsters. Their sinewy bodies and weathered souls became the cogs and gears in the monstrous machinery of a maritime empire, as vast as the unfathomable oceans they traversed. The labour of the lascars—a symphony of sweat, blood, and unyielding perseverance—breathed life into the mighty British merchant fleet. They were the unsung architects of a wealthy realm, their toils casting shadows on the empire's gleaming towers of prosperity.

Among them stood Arun Varma. On the surface, he was a mere cook aboard the HMS Bengal. But delve deeper, and one would find the story of an educated junior clerk from a shipping firm in Chittagong, a man whose sharp intellect and fluency in English set him apart. Dreams of pedagogy and poetry danced in Arun's mind, a future illuminated with promise and aspiration. Yet, the cruel hands of fate had another design. A year prior, the sudden and devastating loss of his father, his beacon, had eclipsed Arun's ambitions. With his dreams now in shadow, responsibility weighed heavily on him. As the family's fulcrum, the responsibility of providing for his grieving mother and three siblings fell squarely on his shoulders. It was amidst this turmoil that Kabir Khan appeared. With sugary promises of prosperity, this agent and overseer whispered of opportunities too tempting for Arun's desperate heart to resist. But unbeknownst to Arun, behind those sweetened words lay chains of bonded labour and a destiny with the East India Company that would alter the course of his life irrevocably.

Arun's memory vividly cradled the indelible first impressions of the day he encountered the HMS Bengal—monumental and foreboding in its stature. Anchored amidst the noisy orchestra of the docks, the ship loomed like a formidable beast, shrouded in an aura of ominous malevolence. The chaotic symphony of the port's hustle and bustle seemed to bow in subtle acquiescence to its imposing presence. Nudged by the relentless hands of destiny, Arun found himself on an irreversible journey as he scuttled up the ship's plank. Arun stood solemnly on the cluttered deck, amidst heaps of tangled ropes and weather-beaten wood. His tall frame navigated the limited space with a quiet grace, his deep-set eyes reflecting the intelligence within. A torrent of emotions surged through him, his stomach churning with anxiety. The world around him seemed blurred, a whirlpool of hurried shadows and sounds as he was swiftly ushered into the mysterious belly of the vessel. It was here, amidst the dim labyrinth of its interior, that the ship unfurled its dark recesses to reveal what would be his new dwelling.

The air within was thick with the essence of exertion and sweat, bearing witness to the multitude of *lascars* already immersed the toil of their work. Blanketed by layers of heat and dust, they moved with a rhythm shaped by necessity, their bodies bending and swaying to the unending tunes of labour, oblivious to Arun's hesitant arrival. Amid this canvas, a commanding shout sliced through the air—Khan's voice, authoritative and unyielding, directing Arun towards his inaugural threshold of duties in the realms of the ship's kitchen. He was greeted with little joy by the others who were busy toiling away in a crammed and stifling hot room where the air was thick with the smell of unwashed bodies, meat and fish entwined with the aromas coming from the pots and pans that were already being used to prepare the next meal.

As the ship set forth on its odyssey, parting from the warm

embrace of his beloved homeland, Arun felt an intimate theatre of terror unfurling within his heart. Each creak and groan of the mighty vessel seemed to reverberate through the chambers of his soul, orchestrating a symphony of trepidation. The arcs of the ship as it navigated through the embracing seas seemed to mirror the undulating waves of anxiety and uncertainty that marked his inner landscape, setting the stage for the unfolding saga of his maritime journey.

Just days into the voyage, Arun began to uncover he harsh truths of life as a lascar aboard the HMS Belfast. Within the heart of this mighty East India ship, stories of adversity and survival echoed through its walls. The seasoned lascars, with hands as rough as the journeys they had endured, painted tales of incredible hardships. Their weathered faces were maps of torturous voyages. Listening to them, Arun felt a wave of respect mixed with sadness. Despite the ruthless treatment they received from the white officers, their spirits remained unbroken, holding onto the hope of a better life with remarkable resilience.

Kabir Khan, the *ghat sarhang*, towered as a formidable figure of authority, enveloping the ship in a rigid aura of dominance with the assistance of his aides, the *tindals*. Their rule infused the ship with a pervasive tension, transforming it into an arena of relentless endurance and determination. Onboard, the lascar's existence was characterised by gruelling labour, a harsh reality that left them broken and vulnerable before their stern superiors. In the beginning, Arun navigated these troubled waters with caution, cultivating strong connections with a handful of lascars and some white sailors within the confines of the kitchens and storerooms. He sought to foster amicable relations universally, focusing particularly on Khan, who regarded him with doubt and distrust. Khan possessed knowledge of Arun's unique background, setting him apart from the other lascars. Arun, with his fluency in English, became the voice of his fellow lascars, acting as a conduit in the tumultuous seas of language and cultural differences that surged across the ship. His linguistic capabilities became a focal point of envy for Khan, who looked upon him with eyes burdened with jealousy and soft-spoken threats carried by the cold winds.

Khan harboured a growing resentment towards Arun during the voyage as Arun's sophisticated manner, evident intelligence and ever-enquiring eyes incessantly irritated Khan, unleashing a surge of jealousy and rage within him. Khan saw himself as the supreme authority among the lascars onboard, treating his words as divine commands to the desperate individuals who shared his heritage, but were, in his eyes, merely his subordinates. Khan wielded his cruelty like a harsh tool to dominate the lascars, forcing them to obey his orders. However, Arun's proficiency in English made him valuable to the British officers, compelling Khan to exercise caution in his dealings with Arun. This limitation only heightened Khan's fury. Khan was solely driven by self-interest, focusing only on amassing wealth for himself, whether it was through gambling, extorting money from other lascars in exchange for favours, or merely serving as a minion to the white Officers. Dominated by greed, Khan was indifferent to the methods he employed, allowing avarice to govern his actions and intentions.

Arun was acutely aware that for himself and many lascars, the journey was a tormenting passage through grave injustice and suffering. Ruthless cruelty stormed their beings with unforgiving fury, leaving in its wake a trail of battered souls and shattered dreams. Despite the trials, dreams of a more promising future imbued Arun and his peers with the resilience and tenacity required to withstand the tribulations of their voyage. However, an unforeseen whirlwind of challenges awaited Arun, a reality he could never have anticipated.

CHAPTER ONE – THE LASH OF THE WINDS & THE WHIP

In the bleak embrace of Victorian London, where cobbled streets whispered with ghostly reverberations and sombre industrial sighs, the formidable HMS Bengal loomed from the horizon, thick fog enveloping its sails as it edged slowly towards the harbour, casting shadows dark as the abyss. This vessel was no mere ship but a guardian of buried truths and a reaper of weary souls. Amidst the melancholic lullabies of the waterways and the shadows of looming spires, this ship, a colossal titan, harboured secrets as deep as the ocean. Each plank upon its deck narrated grim stories of mariners and their shattered hopes, and the eerie phantoms murmuring dark deceptions.

Arun Varma, a gifted lascar hailing from distant Chittagong, sought respite in the melancholic lullabies of the vessel. His days were painted with the aromatic scents of turmeric and cumin as he masterfully curated meals, blending his Indian heritage with the Flavors of the West. But even amidst the rich aromas, Arun's past haunted him. In his ritual of grinding spices, memories ensnared him until a fateful day when James, a curious and jovial cook's mate whom Arun worked with, remarked in his broad Scottish accent, "*ah, turmeric laddie, a treasure from the East.*"

Arun, smiled, but with a sudden haunted gaze, whispered, "*such as with this spice, we are all tethered to the ghost of our birthplace and the lost embrace of our mother.*" James gazed at Arun and with a friendly tap on his back, said, "*aye, we all miss our home. Best gets on with my business.*"

Arun's thoughts went back to the day he had been told by the overseer Kabir Khan who sought him at his home shortly after the death of his father - that working on a ship would bring fortune, a way to pull his family out of the clutches of poverty. When he first set foot on the vessel, he was filled with a mixture of trepidation and excitement. But the novelty soon wore off. Below deck, the boiler rooms were sweltering infernos.

Khan the head overseer, who used his brutality with the lascars as a way of wining favour and special treatment from the white officers. He was a large, barrel-chested man with cold, calculating eyes that missed nothing. A scar ran down one side of his face, a testament to his brutal past. Under his watch, the lascars knew no rest. He took perverse pleasure in their suffering, often pushing them beyond their limits, merely to assert his dominance. One evening, after a particularly gruelling shift, Arun's friend, Akash accidentally spilled curry. Khan, in a fit of rage, lashed out, his whip cutting through the air, leaving a raw, red streak across Akash's back. This was but one of many such instances. The lascars had no voice, no rights. They were simply cogs in a vast, unfeeling machine.

A symphony of creaks and groans filled the ship as it rocked on the angry waves. Below deck, amidst the rancid smell of sweat and damp wood, Arun's ears were haunted by the pitiful moans of bruised bodies and broken spirits. *"This hellish voyage, it's a cursed tomb,"* Mir Jahan, a seasoned *lascar* whispered, his voice trembling like fragile sails in a storm. His face was a canvas of agony, echoing the horrific tales of brutal discipline that left men shattered and spirits broken. One fateful evening, as the tangerine hues of sunset bled into the dark waters, a tumultuous scene unfolded.

Khan, a manifestation of unrestrained fury, surged forth like a monstrous tempest, an embodiment of cruelty and rage. His eyes burned with the fires of hell, and his wrathful hands unleashed a torrent of barbarous blows upon a hapless Muslim lascar, whom for no apparent reason, Khan despised. The air thickened with the torment of a tortured soul, whose agonising cries reverberated through the cursed sails. The stage was set, veiled in the shadows of mercilessness, as Khan, with a heart blackened by sadism, forced upon his victim a vile and abominable sacrilege. The flesh of the forbidden—the unhallowed pork—was thrust with malice into the mouth of the beaten lascar. Each moment, an eternity of humiliation and anguish, savoured by the tormentor as a perverse delight, a culmination of his monstrous theatre of cruelty.

The ship itself seemed to tremble, its timbers echoing the pain and humiliation that tarnished its deck. The other lascars, witnesses to this unforgiving brutality, felt the icy fingers of terror clutch their hearts. In their veins flowed a river of boiling blood and suppressed rage, a tempest constrained by the chains of helpless desperation. Each mind was gripped by the horrific realisation: defiance was the pathway to a merciless abyss, to be consumed by the unforgiving ocean depth as a grotesque spectacle of being thrown overboard, a warning writ in the language of terror for all to see.

Haunted whispers spoke of the nightmarish fates of the vanished souls - lascars who were consumed by the cruel shadows, their existence erased in the heartless expanse of the sea under the malicious gaze of the officers. And so it was that in the dank recesses of the ship, where sunlight rarely reached, Arun and the other lascars found consolation in each other. As days turned to weeks and weeks into months, the brutal reality of their life at sea began to sink in. The long hours and harsh treatment became their daily routine, but amidst the pain, they discovered pockets of joy.

Arun often thought of his family and the woman that he had promised to marry but was forced to leave behind The longing and pain of having left Priya was only soothed by the promise of a better life he was securing for his family. Each blister on his hand, every lash on his back, he bore for them. And as the days grew longer, Arun formed a close bond with Akash, the friend who had been lashed for a mere accident. The two became inseparable, finding strength in each other. Arun's mind recalled one evening, as the ship sailed through the calm waters under a canopy of stars, Arun, Akash, and a few other lascars huddled together on deck.

The night air was cool, a welcome relief from the stifling heat below. They whispered stories of their homes, their families, and their dreams.

Naveen, a young man with a voice like honey, began to sing a melancholic tune that reminded them of their homeland. Soon the others joined in, their voices rising in harmony. It was a song of hope, of longing, and of unity. In that moment, the hardships they faced faded into the background, replaced by a profound connection that tied them together. Kabir Khan, awoken by the melodious tune, peered out of his cabin. Instead of reprimanding them he simply watched, realising, even if just for a moment, that these men were more than just laborers. They were human beings with dreams, hopes, and emotions.

Arun's grasp of English was a rarity among the lascars and gave him a unique place on the ship. The white officers, often finding themselves in need of translation or a bridge between cultures, would summon Arun to mediate. This elevated him in their eyes, and they treated him with a modicum of respect, quite different from the rest of the laborers.

But with this favour came disdain from Kabir Khan. Khan viewed Arun's abilities not as an asset but as a challenge to his authority. The overseer's dominion over the laborers was rooted in maintaining a balance of power, where knowledge and connection to the white officers meant leverage. Arun's literacy and language skills disrupted this balance.

While the other *lascars* admired Arun for his skills, they also recognised the precarious position he was in. He was often caught between his loyalty to his fellow laborers and the expectations of the officers. But Arun, with his quiet strength and integrity, tried to use his unique position for the benefit of all. He would discreetly inform the lascars about the officers' plans, advocate for better conditions, and even sneak extra rations for his mates when he could.

As the days progressed on the voyage, an underlying tension brewed between Khan and Arun. The other *lascars* could feel it, like the static charge before a storm. Whispers circulated about an inevitable confrontation, and bets were placed on outcomes.

One evening, as the sun painted the horizon in hues of gold and crimson, Kabir Khan cornered Arun on the deck, away from prying eyes. *"Why do you think they favour you?"* Khan spat, his eyes cold and unyielding.

Arun, unperturbed, met Khan's gaze. *"It's not favour, Khan. It is respect. Something you can't whip out of someone."*

Khan sneered, his hand inching towards his whip. But before anything could escalate, one of the white officers, called out for Arun. The interruption saved a confrontation, but both men knew this was not the end.

Arun sadly accepted that this was his fate onboard this ship, but that he would calm his soul through memories of home and the friends he had made amongst the other lascars. The lascars realised that they were not alone in their struggle. Together, they could endure, and perhaps, one day, find their way back to the land they called home. Despite the hardships, there was a sense of camaraderie among the men. In their shared suffering, bonds were formed. At night, when the overseers were asleep, they would huddle together, sharing stories from home, singing old songs, and dreaming of a better future. These moments, fleeting as they were, brought solace.

In the oppressive canvas of one monotonous afternoon, where the air was a thick brew of simmering tension, Arun sought refuge in the gentle embrace of cherished memories whilst cooking in the galley kitchen. His mind took flight, navigating through the warm lanes of a life left far behind, wrapped in the tender threads of love and belonging. However, the sanctity of his reminiscence was mercilessly violated as Khan's voice, sharp as a whiplash, ripped through the ambiance with the cruelty of a venomous strike.

Khan stood there, an embodiment of malice, his eyes merciless slits of animosity, each glance a malicious symphony played upon the strings of intimidation. *"What's the delay with the next meal, boy?"* The words slithered from his lips like venomous snakes, hissing threats, and promise of agony. His hand brandished the whip with a sinister finesse, the gleam of its cruel demeanour slicing through the room, foretelling tales of torment.

Within the citadel of Arun's chest, his heart waged a war, the drums of courage battling the relentless strikes of intimidation. Facing Khan's daunting glare, Arun's eyes became the unsung heroes of a silent saga, fortified with the steel of undisputed resilience.

"The food will be ready on time," he said, his voice wrapped in the armour of steadfast determination, masking the turbulent seas of emotions that surged beneath. A silence loomed, heavy with the unspoken battles and looming tempests, as Arun returned to his obligations. But the room remained saturated with the remnants of a hostile encounter, the shadows whispering the unsettling premonitions of forthcoming struggles. Khan, cloaked in the brutal attire of hatred, withdrew into the abyss, leaving behind a trail of muttered obscenities—the grim echoes of an unquenchable fury.

CHAPTER 2: DARKENING HORIZONS

As the sun's dying embers stained the horizon with the last shades of crimson, an ominous gloom crept over the HMS Bengal. The weary laborers felt the weight of more than just their physical exhaustion; an intangible dread seemed to choke the very air they breathed. The officers, usually disciplined and controlled, now radiated tension with tight-lipped silences and curt nods, their eyes darting with suspicion. Captain Sir Reginald Hathaway, once the pillar of strength and resolve, now seemed like a spectre of his former self. His once proud posture was hunched, and his piercing eyes held a haunted look. Shadows played tricks in the dim candlelight as the officers gathered for their nightly game of cards. The sound of shuffling and the occasional clink of a whisky glass were the only respite from the weighty silence.

Leaning in the dank lower deck, Akash's voice, soft and conspiratorial, broke the silence as he whispered to Arun, "*Word is the captain's lost some vital documents. Rumours are swirling about a snake in our midst.*"

Arun stared, open mouthed at his friend Akash. "*What are you talking about?*" he asked with a confused expression.

Akash urged Arun to lower his voice, lest they be heard by the overseer. "*I am just telling you what I heard whilst I was scrubbing the deck. There seem to be a search being conducted by the officers,*" Akash said with a mix of excitement and apprehension. He went on, "*There was a lot of activity around the captain's quarter and Sir Reginald was also pacing around the ship, berating others and shouting at Khan.*"

Arun considered what Akash had told him and decided that discretion was the best course of action. "*Listen my brother,*" he said softly to Akash, "*let's not get involved and do not tell anyone else what you saw or believe has happened."* Looking earnestly at his friend, Arun ended by saying, *"Your curiosity will be your undoing. Now let us get some sleep,"* signally that he did not want to discuss this any further.

The inky darkness outside seemed to mirror the crew's rising apprehensions. But then, breaking through the stifling tension, a scream, so raw and terrifying, echoed through the ship. Every fibre of Arun's being screamed danger, and with wide-eyed horror, he gasped, "*What horror has happened?*"

But before anyone could venture a guess, a cacophony of footsteps, fuelled by panic and fear, thundered towards the deck, racing to confront the unknown terror that awaited them. The suffocating stillness that enveloped the ship was shattered as crew members congregated outside the captain's quarters. Inside lay Sir Reginald, once the commanding presence of the HMS Bengal, now rendered lifeless and pale. His private sanctum, typically a place of order and authority, was transformed into a crime scene. Sir Reginald's bloodied body lay prostrate, his face frozen at death with a look of horror. Alongside the body lay a bloodied knife, confirming the heinous event that took place within his cabin.

"Arun!" cried First Mate Middleton, his voice, loud and quivering with anger. "*Did you see anyone near the captain's chamber?*"

Arun shook his head, his throat dry, "*No, I was in the galley the entire time.*"

However, the murmurs grew louder and more insistent, fuelled by the ominous sight of a knife smeared with blood, found in the very kitchen Arun oversaw. As accusations mounted, the weight of suspicion bore down on him, every glance from the crew seeming to whisper, "*Guilty.*"

Emerging from the crowd, Kabir Khan, with his imposing figure, stepped forward. He locked eyes with Arun, the void of emotion in his gaze making Arun's blood run cold.

"Is this your doing?" Khan's voice was steady, filled with icy disdain.

"I had no hand in this," Arun protested, his voice echoing the desperation he felt. But the dagger's damning presence in his kitchen cornered him in a web of distrust. Even those who had once called him friend now looked at him with doubt and fear.

"I've always served this ship and its crew with loyalty," Arun defended, feeling the weight of the world pressing down on him.

As the intensity of the scene peaked, an officer approached, his demeanour sombre. *"Arun, you are to be confined until a proper investigation can take place."*

The galley that had been Arun's refuge and realm, where he had poured his soul into every meal, now stood as a silent witness to his alleged betrayal.

CHAPTER 3: DAGGER'S SHADOW

A short while later, from the dense curtain of fog that clung to the ship's deck, a tall, imposing figure materialised, instantly arresting everyone's attention. It was Inspector Edwin Blackthorn of Scotland Yard, a detective of such renown that even the hardest of criminals quaked in his presence. His reputation preceded him, and in the dim ship's lanterns, one could see the shadows dance as if hesitant to approach him.

Inspector Blackthorn's tailored charcoal frock coat flapped against his legs, which were clad in creased, dark trousers that disappeared into well-polished boots. His face, marked by a sharp intellect, was framed by a meticulously groomed handlebar Mustache, a style favoured by the discerning gentlemen of the era. A bowler hat sat squarely upon his head, shadowing piercing eyes that seemed to miss nothing. A silver pocket watch, tethered to his waistcoat by a short, ornate chain, was a silent testament to his punctuality and attention to detail. Despite the smog and grime of the city, Inspector Harland maintained a crisp and neat appearance, an unspoken declaration of his steadfast professionalism.

Cutting through the charged atmosphere, Blackthorn's enquiring eyes settled on Arun. His voice, like the cold steel of his demeanour, held a dangerous edge. *"So, a blood-soaked knife in the kitchen of the ship's cook. Is that how the story goes,* lascar?"

Arun's heart raced, his palms sweating. *"Sir, my name is Arun. I am just the cook. I have no knowledge of any bloody knife, nor reason to harm Sir Reginald,"* he managed to stammer out, his voice trembling like leaves in a storm.

Blackthorn took a deliberate step closer, the gap between them seeming to shrink under the weight of his scrutiny. *"Why should*

I believe a word you say?" he questioned, his tone demanding an answer.

Arun gulped hard, trying to summon the words and the courage to speak. "*I've always served faithfully and never harboured resentment against anyone on this ship, let alone Sir Reginald.*"

Standing before this formidable detective, a man whose reputation was whispered about in hushed tones, Arun felt the overwhelming weight of his position—a mere lascar, a servant on a ship, now ensnared in a dark web of suspicion. Every whispered conversation, every glance held potential meaning.

Desperation led Arun to grasp at every memory, seeking a lifeline. He remembered the cryptic conversation he had overheard. "*Inspector,*" Arun began, his voice more confident as he clung to this sliver of information, "*a few nights ago, I overheard Khan speak of a 'lucrative plan'.*" He paused, gathering his thoughts under Blackthorn's unwavering gaze. "*I don't know the specifics, but his tone... it was hushed and urgent, like he was hiding something big.*"

Inspector Blackthorn's face remained inscrutable, but a spark of interest flickered in his eyes. The balance of the narrative was shifting, but where it would land was still uncertain.

"*So, are you saying that this Khan is involved in the murder of Sir Reginald?*" Blackthorn asked calmly while staring deep into Arun's eyes as though he was reading the thoughts in his mind.

Arun considered the question knowing that any open accusation of Khan would only bring him trouble and danger. Feeling unsure and nervous with a pleading look at Blackthorn, Arun said in a quiet voice, "*No Sir, I am not saying that. All I am relating is what I saw and heard. What it means, I cannot say.*"

Blackthorn stood as an unyielding monument of stern inquiry, his stature resonating with the essence of unwavering authority. His eyes, piercing as a falcon focused on a prey, continued to sear at Arun and not acknowledging his answer, rephrased the question.

"So, are you implying that this Khan is entangled in the sinister web of Sir Reginald's murder?" The weight of scrutiny anchored heavily on Arun's shoulders, each second ticking by like a tightening noose of consequential revelations. His mind became a tumultuous sea, where confessions and denials collided with the fierce winds of potential danger and unrest. Knowledge, in this clandestine meeting, became a two-edged sword—its revelations as dangerous as its silence.

"No Sir," Arun's besieging voice emerged from the shadows of reluctance, a soft murmur of reserved discretion, bearing the delicatesse of a petal in a storm. *"I am not affirming such a claim. My words are just a reflection of what I heard."* His words flowed cautiously, like a guarded stream traversing through the rugged terrains of suspicion and reprisal. *"Their implications and interpretations are beyond my wit to surmise"* he added.

The room, in the wake of his words, became a theatre of unplayed dramas and unsung narratives, where the curtains of silence fell heavily upon the stage of undisclosed secrets, leaving behind a lingering aura of mysteries, like smoky trails of an extinguished candle. The space between Blackthorn and Arun vibrated with the silent clashes of the unspoken and the unrevealed, making the atmosphere thick with the echoes of a cryptic overture. The stifling aura of suspicion that encased the room began to wane as Inspector Blackthorn's penetrating gaze upon Arun softened, like the first rays of dawn breaking through a relentless night. It was as though the storm clouds of doubt had momentarily parted, allowing a reluctant beam of understanding to shine through. Yet, Arun's heart continued to palpitate, akin to a caged bird still wary of its surroundings, though sensing an imminent freedom.

While Blackthorn's visage wore the calculated precision of a hawk eyeing its prey, beneath that veneer, Arun perceived an undercurrent of grudging admiration, a ripple in an otherwise unyielding facade. *"You have an eloquent grasp on the Queen's language, Mr. Arun,"* Blackthorn remarked, a hint of genuine astonishment lacing his usually stoic tone.

Arun's throat tightened, the weight of unsung histories and unspoken stories pressing upon him. Clearing his throat gently, he inclined his head, "*My gratitude, Inspector. My father's vision was my compass. He instilled in me the belief that knowledge was both, shield and sword.*" Blackthorn digested Aruns words, unspoken thoughts, his eyes continuing to probe the layers beneath Arun's exterior. "*How does a man of your intellect and upbringing find himself amongst the rugged souls of the HMS Bengal?*"

The unexpected shift into the private terrains of Arun's life felt like a gale sweeping through a tranquil meadow. Caught in the crosswinds of surprise and nostalgia, Arun took a fleeting moment, gathering his memories like treasured relics, before embarking on a journey into his past. With a voice that echoed the cadence of ancient tales and the melodies of lost dreams, Arun unfurled the tapestry of his life — the grandeur of his childhood, his father's soaring aspirations, and the cruel twist of fate that anchored him aboard the forlorn decks of the HMS Bengal. With each word, each nuance, Blackthorn seemed to be drawn deeper into the narrative, the Inspector's stern exterior melting under the warmth of Arun's candid revelations.

The ship's timbers creaked, echoing the tense atmosphere in the room. After Arun's recount, the room's air grew thick with silence. The two men locked eyes, both searching for truth and clarity. Inspector Blackthorn finally spoke, addressing both Arun and the constables that flanked him.

"*Mr. Arun, I would like your assistance in this investigation. Your linguistic capabilities and familiarity with the crew could prove invaluable.*" A rush of hope surged within Arun, only to be doused by Blackthorn's cautionary continuation. "*However, let's be clear. My trust is not easily earned, and this is as much about keeping you within my sights as it is about your utility.*"

Arun tried to decipher the man before him. Was that a faint hint of a smile, of assurance perhaps? Or just a trick of the dim lighting? It was hard to tell with a man as enigmatic as Inspector Edwin Blackthorn and whose face seemed to be chiselled out of granite.

CHAPTER 4: TWIST OF FATE

In the dimly lit confines of the captain's quarters aboard the HMS Bengal, Inspector Blackthorn, with a determined countenance, voiced a most unconventional request. "*I want Arun off this ship and under my custody. H is imperative to my investigation.*"

First Mate Chief Middleton, second in command and a seasoned mariner with lines of experience etched deep on his face, looked askance at the detective. "*That's highly irregular, Inspector. What warrants such a demand?*" His voice dripping with irritation.

Blackthorn paused, taking a moment to phrase his thoughts and ignoring the barbed tone of the captain's response. "*I've investigated numerous cases in my time, Mr Middleton. But there is something here, an undercurrent that I cannot quite put my finger on. And my gut tells me that Arun is right at the heart of it.*"

Middleton stared at the Inspector, his face still showing indignation, replied curtly, "*I still do not see why you need Arun's assistance. "His duty is to the ship,*" he said forcibly.

Blackthorn took a deep breath to compose himself and leaned forward, hands flat on the polished oak table. "*Mr Middleton, Arun's presence on this ship, in the wake of the murder and that damned bloodied knife, paints a target on his back. It is not just about keeping an eye on him. It's about ensuring his safety from any unsolicited reprisals.*"

Middleton finally relented, feeling a mixture of boredom and superiority, he simply said, "*Do what you must then Inspector, I have urgent duties to attend to. As you can appreciate, this is a distressing time for the crew,*" his voice condescending in its tone.

Arun, standing by the door and eavesdropping on the conversation, felt a mix of trepidation and wonder. He had come to expect being overlooked, being just another Lascar, a mere footnote in the vast canvas of shipboard life. Yet here he was, a pivotal character in a twisted narrative.

When news of the decision reached him, his heart raced. He would be billeted ashore, in a world far removed from the swaying decks and salty spray. And more intriguingly, he would be walking side by side with the legendary Inspector Blackthorn, a man whose stories of cunning and resolve were whispered in awe across London's alleys and taverns.

The weight of the situation pressed upon Arun, but an ember of anticipation flickered within. This unexpected twist of fate was the key to proving his innocence, to reclaiming his name, and to embarking on a journey of truth amidst treacherous waters.

CHAPTER 5: UNCHARTERED WATERS

As Arun stepped forth from the shadowy embrace of the murky docks, his soles gently caressed the ancient, time-worn cobblestones of Victorian London. A mighty gust of icy wind swept through the labyrinthine streets, its frosty arms encircling him in a steely embrace that stood in stark contrast to the nurturing warmth of the soft breezes in his distant homeland.

The bustling symphony of the metropolis came alive around him, a rich and overwhelming tapestry woven with the threads of a thousand distinct sounds. Shouts and the robust bartering of market vendors rang in the air, their voices echoing off the soot-covered walls of grandiose buildings, creating a resonant chorus of commerce. The rhythmic, insistent clatter of horse hooves upon stone resonated through the misty air, a steady drumbeat that underscored the melody of the city's ceaseless motion. From the hidden corners and unseen alleyways, the effervescent giggles and laughter of children fluttered, an incongruent but life-affirming refrain amidst the symphony of the urban theatre.

Arun moved with cautious curiosity, each step an exploration, as he navigated through the omnipresent aromas that seemed to seep from the very soul of London. The pungent odour of dung, left in the wake of passing carriages, lingered heavily on the cobblestoned pathways, mingling in a robust olfactory dance with the smoky breath of the city. Myriad scents floated on the crisp air: the rich, warm aroma of freshly baked bread wafting from the doors of bustling bakeries; the heady and intoxicating allure of spices and exotic fragrances that drifted from apothecaries and the open doors of busy inns; the sharp tang of sweat and the musky essence of the unwashed masses that permeated the crowded byways and bustling thoroughfares.

Each corner held the whispers of countless tales, in the rustling of the ladies' silken gowns, and in the hushed conversations that flickered like candle flames in the dimly lit doorways of ancient alehouses. The cobbled streets echoed with the vibrant chatter of life, each footfall, every rustle of fabric, and every muted conversation contributing to the vivid, ever-changing portrait of Victorian London, in which Arun now found himself an enigmatic wanderer.

As he ambled through the sprawling streets, with their stately townhouses and majestic cathedrals, Arun's traditional attire — a vibrant kurta and a turban — attracted more than a few glances. Many were simply curious, their eyes reflecting the wonder of seeing a world they had only heard tales of. But intertwined with these inquisitive looks were others, darker and disdainful.

At a bustling market square, where the marketplace throbbed with a myriad of sights, sounds, and exchanges, Arun found himself momentarily ensnared by the colourful tapestry of commerce, which remined him of the markets back home in Chittagong. The square bustled with a lively chaos, alive with the rough melodies of haggling and the robust chorus of merchants peddling their exotic wares. Here, fruits gleamed like precious jewels beneath the muted grey skies, their vivid hues a silent testament to faraway lands.

Amidst this mosaic of life, a fruit vendor, with a face weathered by many a biting English winter, cast a snide remark towards his neighbour, a shadow of mockery cloaking his words. *"Look at that! An Indian prince, lost in London, I wager!"* he jeered, his voice heavy with a derision as thick as London's infamous fog.

His companion, a rough-hewn symphony of laughter erupting from his chest, played along with a sarcastic bow and a theatrically embellished, *"What will you like, guv?"*

Their laughter, a discordant melody in the marketplace opera, grated against Arun's ears like the screeching of a rusty hinge. Nonetheless, Arun mustered the grace to adorn his lips with a courteous smile, offering a placating *"greetings,"* which only fanned the flames of their mirth.

Meandering through the dim and secluded alleys, where the cobblestones echoed with the ghosts of a thousand footfalls, Arun encountered a tableau of childhood. Here, amidst the grime and the dust that seemed as much a part of London as its majestic Thames, children, their faces a canvas of street dust and playful innocence, were engrossed in the timeless art of marbles. A whirlpool of giggles and mischief encircled Arun as the children, in their innocent cruelty, morphed into mockingbirds, mimicking his accent with exaggerated theatricality.

"Look at 'is clothes, mate, is he lost from the circus!" jested a boy, his eyes twinkling with the mischievous spark of youth. A playful breeze carried the bouncing giggles and bobbing pigtails of a young girl who added, *"Speak English, why don't ya!"*

A corner turned brought with it an encounter with age, embodied in an elderly woman. Draped in the shawls of mistrust, she manoeuvred through the murky streets, her spine bowed in submission to the passage of time, but her hand resolute in its grasp upon her handbag. Suspicion lurked within the depths of her pale, watchful eyes, and as she crossed paths with Arun, the shadows of prejudice tightened her grip, causing her frail form to hasten its retreat.

However, amidst the prickle of prejudice, there were glimmers of warmth. A few streets down, the tantalising scent of old books drew Arun into a cozy bookstore. The proprietor, an affable man with spectacles perched on his nose, struck up a conversation. *"Your attire is quite distinct,"* he remarked genuinely. As Arun shared tales of Indian folklore and traditions, the owner's face lit up. *"How fascinating! Join me for tea, won't you? I'd love to hear more."*

Further along, outside a shop with mannequins donning the

latest London fashion, a seamstress paused in her work, captivated by the embroidery on Arun's kurta.

"The detailing is impeccable," she said, eyes wide with appreciation. "*I've never seen anything like it here. Would you mind if I had a closer look?*" Arun looked at her and moved towards her with a smile and with a warm smile responded, "*please be my guest.*"

Arun's initial trepidation began to fade as he walked the maze-like streets of Victorian London. He quickly grasped that for all its vastness, the city was much like a quilt – some patches might be frayed or worn, but others gleamed brightly, fresh and vibrant. And he, with his unique culture and history, was now a part of it.

The pervasive fog that hung over London, mysterious and thick, seemed to mirror Arun's dramatic journey on the HMS Bengal. And just as he had found his way aboard the ship, he was resolute in carving out a space for himself amidst the teeming throngs of the English capital. Alongside, Blackthorn remained silent and passive as he observed Arun and noted the reaction from others to him with a blend of fascination and admiration. The edges of his mouth subtly curved, imperceptibly, betraying a whisper of emotion as he studied the reactions of the populace to the exotic presence of his companion.

Blackthorn, his voice emerging as a gravelly murmur, woven into the fabric of the fog-laden air, "*tell me, Arun, what visions occupy your mind as you traverse the pathways of this metropolis?*"

Arun, turning towards his companion, his eyes reflecting the glow of the lanterns flickering in the night, "Inspector Blackthorn," his voice carrying the melodies of his Indian origins, "*this city, shrouded in mysteries, is like a cryptic manuscript. Each corner is inscribed with tales yet to unveil themselves to my eager eyes.*"

Blackthorn, nodding, his gaze steadfast on Arun's face, seeking to decipher the tales hidden within his expressions, "*you carry yourself with a calm that is as baffling as it is profound. Despite the tribulations of your journey and your current whereabouts, you seem still in wonder of your new surroundings. What keeps the flame of your curiosity and wonder burning so vibrantly?"*

A smile, soft as the silken threads of Eastern tales, played upon Arun's lips. *"One must embrace the symphony of existence,"* he said, *his words flowing like a gentle river of wisdom. "Each moment, each obstacle, is but a note in this grand composition. In the embrace of the unknown, I find the rhythms of wonder and exploration."* Blackthorn smiled at Arun and said, *"you are quite the Poet Arun!"* And with that, Blackthorn and Arun walked on in silence through the cold and fog laden streets of Victorian London.

After navigating the labyrinthine, gas-lit lanes of Victorian London, Blackthorn guided Arun on a quest to find him shelter against the biting cold. The rhythmic patter of their shoes on the rain-slick cobblestones was occasionally interrupted by the sharp clack of horse hooves and distant murmur of tavern conversations. Each doorway of a Tavern or Hostel they approached with hope, only to be met with thinly veiled contempt or outright hostility, became a stark reminder of the city's underlying prejudices.

Blackthorn's frustration grew palpable with each rebuff. After being dismissed curtly by a landlord whose nose wrinkled in apparent distaste, he turned to Arun, exhaling sharply. *"It's not just your appearance, Arun,"* he said with a mix of irritation and sympathy. *"It's the deep-rooted misconceptions that taint their views."*

The shadows emphasised the worry lines on his face. *"I always knew there were ignorant people amongst all classes, but I genuinely believed London to be more progressive, more accepting and modern. Perhaps I've been naive."* *"Come let's keep going,"* he said in a solemn voice and the next landlord that they encountered pushed Blackthorn to the edge of his professionalism.

It was on one vile murky street of Victorian London, where the wind carried whispers of unsolved mysteries and the cobblestones were drenched in the shadows of the unknown, Blackthorn and Arun found themselves standing before the ominous threshold of a dilapidated tavern. Upon knocking upon a creaking Tavern with a sign saying 'lodging available' hanging above, they were confronted by a heavily built middle aged man with grubby, stained apron stretched to its limited around in huge belly.

He stared at Blackthorn and Arun, his eyes narrowing on the dark stranger. "*How do*" he grunted without any sign of warmth or welcome in this bitter night.

"*I am Inspector Blackthorn" and this is Arun Varma who is assisting me on a case. I need a room for him for a few nights*" said Blackthorn in his most official sounding voice.

The cavernous room behind the hulking frame of the Landlord seemed to hold its breath, waiting, watching as the landlord's eyes danced with shadows of cruelty and bigotry. His words, a venomous concoction of malice and sadistic pleasure, lashed through the grimy air, rejecting them with a scornful emphasis on Arun's foreign origins.

With obvious indifference to Blackthorns request and a cold glance at Arun, he turned to Blackthorn, "*I'm sorry guv we have no room, especially for a coolie*" he said with a sadistic smile. Blackthorn took a deep breath to calm the growing anger inside him and composed himself once more.

"*Listen to my words,* Landlord," Blackthorn commenced, his tone draped in a tapestry of stern authority and veiled implications. "*I have no desire to scrutinise this establishment with the piercing eye of officialdom,*" he articulated, knowing from experience the swathes of illegality that took place in the dark recesses of taverns such as this.

"However, I find myself compelled to inquire once more: are there any chambers within this place that remain unclaimed?" The landlord's visage unfurled into a sinister smirk, and from the depths of his throat emanated a growl, coarse and steeped in scorn. *"As the master of this house,"* he began, his words thick with mockery and the bitter residue of disrespect, growled with a smirk, *"I have the legal right to let anyone in or refuse someone and no law says any different, so with all due respect, you can both piss off Inspector"* he said defiantly.

A tempest stirred within Blackthorn, the tumultuous seas of anger and frustration threatening the shores of his professionalism. The evening, marred by the unforgiving cold and a labyrinth of rejections, had eroded his patience, leaving in its wake a raw, exposed nerve. The landlord's sneering defiance was the bitter gust that unleashed the storm.

Blackthorn losing all sense of control and his anger lunged and grabbed the landlord by the neck, pushing him roughly into the centre of the Tavern. The bar went instantly quiet with all eyes on Blackthorn and the Landlord. *"Listen you fat fucker, don't you ever speak to a Scotland Yard Detective in that manner, or I will throw you in the cell and close this place down".*

Darkness fell upon the tavern, an ominous silence weaving through the hazy lamplight as Blackthorn, embodying the fierce tempest of justice and wrath, unleashed the storm of punches and then hands, wrought with the fury of righteous anger, found the thick, vile neck of the bigot, propelling him violently over the grimy bar. Shadows and whispers retreated to the corners, and the room bore witness to the raw, unmasked face of the Inspectors rage.

Blackthorn had his hands around the throat of the Landlord and was squeezing hard making the landlord's face turn pink and purple. In a frenzy of desperation, the landlord's hands clawed at

Blackthorn's unyielding grip, a chaotic dance of survival played out in the dim, murky light of the tavern. The desperate gasps for breath echoed through the silence, each moment intensifying the grim spectacle.

Arun, witnessing the terrifying transformation of the landlord's visage under the merciless hold of Blackthorn's hands, surged forward, propelled by a sense of urgency.

"Inspector Blackthorn, Sir!" his voice resonated through the tense air, imbued with an impassioned plea. *"Desist, I beseech you, sir! This man, wretched though he may be, surely does not warrant injury or worse?"*

The gallery of faces within the tavern watched a symphony of raised eyebrows and muted gasps marking the unexpected intervention. Whispers adorned the thick air as onlookers found themselves bewildered, not merely by the spectacle of unfolding conflict, but also by the eloquence of the English tongue as wielded by the dark stranger. In the tumultuous arena of strained breaths and raging emotions, the clear note of Arun's urgent appeal struck a chord within Blackthorn.

A moment of clarity shone through the red fog of rage, guiding Blackthorn's professional integrity back to the fore. He loosened his vice like grip on the Landlords neck, letting his bulbous body to collapse in a heap of ragged breaths and trembling flesh upon the floor. Blackthorn's eyes, dark pools swirling with storms of conflicted emotions, lingered over the dejected form of the landlord before sweeping across the room, capturing the silent, watchful occupants of the murky tavern.

Turning with a swift, decisive motion, he nodded subtly to Arun, a silent command reverberating through the tense space, *"Let us remove ourselves from this cesspit,"* his words echoed, carrying the weight of unspoken disdain.

In tandem, they traversed towards the exit, each step a silent echo reverberating through the chamber, leaving behind the shadows of confrontation to be consumed by the tavern's ominous embrace. A wordless symphony played between them as they moved through the chilly night, allowing the icy winds to sweep away the tumultuous remnants of the conflict. Arun, embodying a serene understanding, allowed silence to be their companion, giving space for Blackthorn's internal tempest to find its calm, letting the waves of anger dissolve into the night's embrace.

Blackthorn, enshrouded in a cloud of introspection, found himself journeying through the conflicted passages of his own mind. A torrent of questions raged each thought clashing against the rocks of doubt and self-examination - was it a fiery defence of personal respect, or a vehement outcry against the venomous fangs of prejudice that had dared to bare themselves? The answers remained shrouded in the murky veils of introspection, leaving Blackthorn with a feeling of guilt and pride.

Through the frost-kissed alleys they walked, a silence heavy with the weight of unspoken words and unanswered questions enveloping them. Arun looked to the fog-draped spires and towering structures around them, feeling the weight of centuries of history and prejudice.

His eyes met Blackthorn's, showing a well of comprehension and fortitude and said softly. *"Similar prejudices persist in my own land as well. The world is immense, but often, minds prove to be incredibly narrow."*

Blackthorn gave a subdued nod, only half-listening, his annoyance simmering, visible in the rigid set of his jaw and the furrow of his brows. The renowned detective, usually a staunch advocate for justice, now found himself wrestling with the deep-seated biases of society.

As they moved forward, the narrow streets cast shadows that echoed their shared isolation. Blackthorn's hand, which had always been more accustomed to wielding a weapon or clutching evidence, found its way onto Arun's shoulder. It was an act neither of protection nor of reassurance but of genuine camaraderie. The moment spoke volumes. The night's experiences were proving to be an awakening for Blackthorn, making him confront the unsettling undercurrents in the very society he had pledged to serve.

Blackthorn glanced sidelong at Arun, noticing the gentle set of his jaw and the quiet resilience in his eyes, eyes that spoke of ancient cultures and vast landscapes, eyes that had witnessed both the wonders and cruelties of life. Here was a man who, despite being thrust into an unfamiliar world that frequently rebuffed him, still held onto his dignity and grace.

"*Arun,*" Blackthorn began, his voice softer than usual, "*I can't begin to fathom the depths of the trials you face daily in this land but know this – I'm honoured to walk beside you.*"

Arun smiled faintly, his eyes reflecting a myriad of emotions. "*In every land and every era, there are battles to be fought, Inspector. Mine might be more evident, but we all have our struggles.*" "*From the shadowed decks of the ship, I placed you on the same pedestal as those white officers. In their eyes, I was naught but a mere whisper above the beasts of the fields,*"

Arun's voice held a restrained passion, each word heavy with memories of pain and prejudice. Blackthorn's face flushed, a turbulent mix of surprise and indignation. For a heartbeat, anger threatened to break free, but he swallowed hard, forcing himself to truly hear the weight and truth of Arun's confession.

The two men shared a moment of mutual understanding, both recognising that beneath the layers of duty, culture, and skin, lay shared human experiences and vulnerabilities. They were, in many ways, reflections of each other – bound by circumstance, yet growing together in respect and recognition.

CHAPTER 6: EARTH

In the dimmed labyrinth of London's streets, a solitary beacon of warmth beckoned them—a quaint inn nestled close to the docks. Its windows glowed with a gentle light, and through its cracks, the soft hum of merriment and laughter promised a respite from the coldness they had faced thus far. The inn's wooden door, aged and worn, creaked open to reveal a bustling world inside. In its midst, a young woman with eyes that sparkled like the first stars of twilight and a smile that radiated genuine warmth, stepped forward.

"Inspector Blackthorn, how lovely to see you Sir" she said with feeling. Her presence was like a balm, and Blackthorn's shoulders, hunched from the evening's stresses, seemed to relax a fraction.

"Emily," he began, his voice tinged with unmistakable gratitude, "this weary traveller beside me is Arun. The city has not been kind to us tonight. Might you have a room to spare for him?"

Emily's only then noticing Arun, looked at him with a mixture of curiosity and surprise. She looked at the dusky colour of his skin, his big eyes and thick black hair.

"Hello Arun, it good to meet you" she said, unsure whether this exotic looking man understood what she was saying. Arun looked at her and gave a warm smile, his white teeth radiating in the dim light. *"It's a pleasure to meet you"* he said, relieved at finally receiving a warm human welcome.

Emily's response was immediate, her hand reaching out to grasp Arun's in a gesture that was both welcoming and comforting. *"Arun,"* she began, her voice soft yet firm, " welcome, *you will find no trouble or hate here. Anyone vouched for by Inspector Blackthorn is family to us."* The weight that Arun had carried, evident in his wary gaze, seemed to lighten just a touch.

Following a modest yet satisfying repast of crusty bread, rich cheese, and a generous helping of ale, the atmosphere of the room was filled with a warm, congenial aura. Blackthorn, after a moment of contemplative silence, prepared to take his leave. He turned towards Arun, his demeanour a harmonious blend of authority and genuine concern. His words flowed with the assured cadence of an Inspector, reflecting the facets of his professional persona. *"Arun,"* he said with a calm yet purposeful tone, *"I shall see you at the break of dawn tomorrow. I suggest you get a good night's sleep as tomorrow will now doubt bring a day of toil and hopefully success."*

Arun absorbed Blackthorn's words, allowing them to plant seeds of assurance and determination within his tired spirit. With a gesture of respect and gratitude, he straightened his posture, rising to stand firmly within the space. His voice carried threads of appreciation woven with the soft textures of vulnerability.

"I thank you for your kindness and in finding me this place of solace," he said, allowing the sincerity of his words to paint the room with hues of gratitude.

Blackthorn responded with a nod, an unspoken symphony of understanding and camaraderie playing in the simple gesture. His form then receded into the night, leaving behind an ambiance of silent promises and the subtle echoes of a day that had woven threads of various human spirits into the intricate tapestry of life's ongoing saga.

As the night unfolded within the protective embrace of the inn's walls, Emily, a kitchen maid, began to sense a bond with Arun, who appeared adrift in an unfamiliar land. Life had dealt Emily its share of adversity—she had weathered the hardship of losing her parents to poverty and consumption. Emily had diligently worked her way up to her current position, considering herself fortunate; life could have dragged her into the bleak alleyways of London, where survival often meant resorting to crime or enduring a life of ignominy and exploitation. Her shared experience of struggle fostered a feeling of connection with Arun, allowing empathy to bridge the distance between two souls navigating the harsh landscapes of their lives.

Emily and Arun delved deep into tales of their lives. In the flickering candlelight, they traded stories: Arun, with his tales of vibrant Indian festivals, of rains that danced on terracotta roofs, of ancient temples echoing with timeless prayers; and Emily, with her narratives of fog-kissed London mornings, the cacophony of its markets, and the mysteries the Thames whispered every dawn. In the tapestry of their exchanged stories, they unearthed a universal truth: that beneath the myriad shades of skin, the lilts of different tongues, and the intricacies of diverse traditions, human hearts beat in rhythm to the same timeless melodies of joy, sorrow, and longing. As Emily spoke, Arun was reminded of the cadence of another voice he once held dear. It had been an age since he had conversed deeply with a woman, and while Emily's words were a balm to his soul, they also pierced the tender scar of memories he had kept sheltered for so long.

His mind travelled miles away, to sun-kissed riverbanks in Bengal, where he once sat beside his beloved Priya. They would lose themselves in discussions of profound poetry, dreams woven in golden threads, and the myriad pathways their futures could take. Priya's laughter was the song he yearned to hear, her gaze the sanctuary he sought in moments of solitude. The pursuit of a better life, one free from the chains of poverty and where he could honour his father's legacy, had drawn him away from her embrace.

Tonight, under the vast umbrella of the night sky, Emily's words subtly danced through the delicate fabric of time and space, intertwining the rugged cobblestones of London with the ethereal sands beside Bengal's mystical rivers. The room seemed to resonate with the silent echoes of lands far away, carrying the fragrance of memories—some sweet whispers of joy, others echoing the depths of lost moments and bygone days. As the soft luminescence of the lamp flickered, casting enigmatic shadows that seemed to tell tales of a realm forgotten, Emily's gentle conversation wrapped itself around Arun's soul. Her words, woven with tender threads of understanding and care, ushered in waves of nostalgia, allowing the essence of far-off riversides to permeate the confining walls, momentarily bridging the vast distances that life's journeys had created.

Seeing Arun lost in a sea of distant thoughts, Emily's eyes shimmered with empathy. A silent understanding lingered in the space between words and breaths.

She hesitated, choosing her words with the care of one who steps tenderly upon a path strewn with delicate blossoms. *"Is everything alright, Arun?"* she asked softly, her voice weaving a warm tapestry of comfort within the chilly room. Arun's eyes met hers, heavy with the weight of unshed tears and stories yet untold. A small, appreciative smile graced his lips as he nodded silently, feeling the quiet strength of companionship amidst the echoing silence of solitude.

"I'm managing, truly," he murmured gently, the soft undulations of his voice bearing the weight of a heart heavy with nostalgia. *"Forgive me, the day's occurrences have left me somewhat weary, and my thoughts seem to find solace in the warm embrace of my distant homeland."*

His words lingered in the room, like delicate traces of a long-lost fragrance, weaving the essence of faraway places into the fabric of the present. Emily's eyes met his, shimmering pools of empathy and understanding reflecting the soft flickers of the dimming light. Her voice, tender as the touch of a soothing breeze, carried words that resonated with the subtleties of heartfelt care.

"It must be so hard," she said softly, allowing her words to flow like a gentle stream of comfort, *"being away from the embrace of your home, and the warmth of your people."* She hesitated slightly, her

words steeped in the gentle essence of empathy, allowing space for his vulnerability to breathe.

Arun's eyes softly embraced Emily's presence. In her, beauty manifested not as a mere alignment of features, but as an aura, a warm luminescence that was woven from threads of kindness and a sincere curiosity for the diverse tapestry of life and cultures. Her spirit seemed to glow with a warm light, enhancing her appeal with an ethereal charm that was far removed from the conventional realms of physical allure. Her willingness to voyage through different worlds, embracing the myriad hues and rhythms of various cultures, added a richness to her essence, making her presence feel like a warm, comforting melody that soothed the heart's hidden aches. In her, he found a gentle harbour where stories and emotions could unfold freely, weaving strands of connection that eased the heaviness of distance and longing.

Emily gently touched his arm, her touch a soft echo of comfort. *"I think it's time to rest, it's been a long day,"* she suggested kindly. *"there's nothing like a good night's sleep to wash away your troubles."* *"I'll head to my room now and hope the morrow brings you some peace"* she continued, standing up gracefully, letting the fabric of her presence gently fall away from the room's atmosphere.

And with that, she moved towards the door, leaving behind a comforting silence, as if her words had softly caressed the harsh edges of reality, leaving behind a gentle cascade of hope and warmth. Alone again, Arun felt a subtle comfort lingering in the room, a quiet testament to the compassionate exchange. The embrace of the night seemed a bit softer, the shadows whispering not just of loneliness but also of a shared understanding and a hope that, in the heart of night's silence, sleep could bring solace to a heart heavy with the echoes of distant shores and untraveled paths.

CHAPTER 7: FIRE

A piercing ray of sunlight filtered through the curtains, rudely rousing Arun from his slumber. But it was not just the early morning light that woke him – the shadow of Inspector Blackthorn loomed over him; his countenance hardened like forged steel. Every line on Blackthorn's face spoke of an unwavering commitment, an unyielding pursuit of justice that had become his hallmark. The weight of the looming investigation was palpable.

"Time to rise, Arun," Blackthorn's voice held a hint of urgency. *"Get dressed. We've a full day ahead."*

Within minutes, Arun found himself seated across from the inspector over a breakfast of bread of cheese, the dimly lit room casting elongated shadows on the wooden floor. Blackthorn meticulously laid out their agenda, methodically tracing out their steps. Their primary task? Delve into the ship's secrets - its crew, the hidden nooks of its cargo, and every whispered legend that accompanied it.

For Arun, however, the prospect was not just about uncovering secrets. It was personal. Blackthorn needed him to bridge the linguistic gap, to converse with the lascars, many of whom had been silent witnesses to the sinister events that fatal night. Anxiety gnawed at Arun's gut, intertwining with the adrenaline rush of this newfound responsibility. How would the lascars, his brethren, perceive his newfound alliance? However, he also held onto the hope that their collective fear of Khan would be overshadowed by their thirst for justice.

Sensing Arun's internal turmoil, Blackthorn leaned forward, his blue eyes searching Arun's. *"Listen, Arun,"* he began, his voice softer, *"Khan and his cohorts? They are my territory. Let me handle them. Your focus is on getting the truth from the* lascars."

A hint of a reassuring smile played on Blackthorn's lips, though Arun could not fully shake off his apprehensions. He swallowed hard, giving a brief nod of acknowledgment, hoping that the day would bring them closer to the truth that seemed ever so elusive.

The morning unfurled its grey veils across the London sky, wrapping the city in a soft, fog-kissed embrace, a muted ballet of shadows and light playing upon the ancient cobblestones. With hearts pulsing with the rhythms of hope and the subtle echoes of anticipation weaving through their steps, Blackthorn and Arun stood before the looming edifice of the East India Company offices. A majestic canvas of architecture, the building wore gilded signs and fluttering British flags like jewels, each element narrating tales of imperial grandeur and echoes of a powerful legacy. Within the opulent embrace of the halls, richly bathed in the hues of affluence and authority, they embarked on their quest for knowledge. But their journey through the labyrinth of bureaucracy was met with walls of refusal, as unyielding as the high, stern wooden counters that adorned the space. Clerks, armed with quills and guarded by ink pots, stood like sentinels of information, their faces etched with the unyielding lines of protocol. At every turn, their request for information was met with a stony silence, culminating in a senior clerk demanding that they submit a formal writ to secure the information they wanted.

Their spirits, though brushed by the cold winds of disappointment, were not to be deterred. With a quiet resilience, they stepped into the maze-like embrace of London's East End, where the streets whispered secrets in the language of grimy cobblestones and laundry lines that swayed like ancient scrolls of untold stories. In this theatre of shadows, where the alleyways pulsed with the vibrant, chaotic rhythms of black-market symphonies, their senses were embraced by a myriad of elusive melodies and hidden harmonies. The murky corners were inhabited by hawkers, fences, and harbour gangs, each figure a guarded keeper of clandestine tales. Eyes, veiled with the cloaks of suspicion and mystery, met theirs, but unveiled no secrets, sharing no whispered symphonies of hidden truths or unveiled paths through the landscapes of uncertainty.

"Inspector Blackthorn," murmured Arun, the words almost lost amidst the cacophony from the surrounding industry of people, animals and dingy stalls and alleyways. *"This place, it's like a labyrinth of hidden secrets and vices."*

Blackthorn nodded, his experienced eyes scanning the darkling theatre around them. *"Indeed, Arun. Here, in these veiled arteries of London lies the heart of its underbelly of crime and deception"* he said in a matter-of-fact tone.

In a dimly lit corner, where the soft glow of a lantern tenderly embraced the cobblestones, stood a hawker. His wares unfurled before him, a forbidden treasure to behold, no doubt acquired from raping several wealth homes of their possessions.

"Good evening, sirs," he greeted, his voice a soft zephyr amidst the underworld's simmering tempest. *"Tonight's offerings are from all corners of the Empire, you won't see such trinkets and treasures anywhere else gentleman"* he said with a smile.

Blackthorn, his visage etched with lines of wisdom and discernment, inched closer, absorbing the words in the silent corridors of comprehension. *"Listen, we are in search of any information you may know about the incomings and outgoings from the Harbour,"* he said, his voice subtly navigating the paths of question and reverence.

"You look like a fellow with his ears to the ground. Do you know which elusive ships and cargos find their way to these parts? He said casually.

The hawker's eyes dimmed with caution, a guarded shroud obscuring the hidden realms within. *"So, you must be a copper then?"* he said accusingly. *And who is the hell is this Blackamore with you*? *I have seen his kind at the docks, why do not you ask him, his lot are always thieving!"* He said sharply.

Blackthorn ignored the question, fighting back the irritation from the Hawkers barbed comments about Arun, knowing he had to tread carefully in order not to scare away the hawkers. *"Listen my man, I mean you no harm. I just want to know who I should be speaking with to know what happens at the Dock"* he said calmly.

"Why?" asked the Hawker, *"I earn and honest living guv."* Controlling his frustration, Blackthorn sighed, *"I am not questioning your trade, nor do I care where your goods come from. All I want is to be pointed in the direction of someone who can assist me in a murder case"* he said.

The Hawker eyes grew wide at the mention of Murder and seemed to backway from Blackthorn, his eyes darting between Blackthorn and Arun in panic. *"I don't know nothing about a murder guv"* he said nervously and *"I know no names of people that may know"* he added. *"I just want to be left alone"* he said, looking all around him now as though he was being watched.

Blackthorn sighed and realised that there was nothing more to be gained out of this man. As Blackthorn was about to walk away, he was stopped when Arun walked up to the Hawker and enquired about his goods.

"There are some fine pieces here" he observed, flashing a warm smile at the Hawker.

The Hawker was speechless for a moment, astounded by the polished words spoken by this dark stranger. "Nothing but the very best" the Hawker muttered, trying to compose himself.

Arun went onto examine some of the items, inquiring about their origins and authenticity. *"Some of these items reminds me of home"* Arun said, *"fine craftsmanship"* he continued, *"can you get more of these, I may have a buyer for you,"* he said to the Hawker.

The Hawker now wrapped with curiosity and spurned by greed, responded with an emphatic, *"yes, I can get more, if you have the money,"* staring at Arun. *"How do you get hold of these goods, I need to ensure they are genuine,"* Arun stated in a business manner.

"They are genuine Mister," the Hawker replied, *"I'm known in these parts and deal with all the ships that come in."* Arun exchanged a glance with Blackthorn with a slight hint of a smile.

"Thank you, Sir, I will return to you to purchase some of the items, will you still be here in a day or so?" Arun said to the Hawker. The Hawker narrowed his eyes, but the temptation of a potential sale, pushed aside any suspicions of Arun, *"well I can't say if any of what you liked will still be here, but this stall will be here."*

Arun nodded at the man and turned to Blackthorn, with a look that suggested they walk on. Blackthorn looked at the Hawker and then nodded to Arun to move on. Blackthorn said nothing until they were out of ear shot from the Hawker and turned to Arun.

Looking at him with air of curiosity, Blackthorn said, *"well what was that all about Arun?"* Arun wondering whether he had overstepped the mark with the Inspector, composed himself and said, *"whilst you were speaking with the Hawker, I looked at the goods on his stall and noticed some of them. They were from my ship, and I had seen some of them being packed and unloaded"* he said looking at Blackthorn.

Understanding beginning to wash over Blackthorns face. *"I hope you did not mind, but I wanted to find out from the Hawker where he had acquired the goods and did so in a way that didn't alert him to my intentions"* said Arun, hoping he had done the right thing.

A smile formed on Blackthorns face as he comprehension of Aruns actions sunk in. *"You, clever rascal"* Blackthorn said with a beaming smile on his face. *"By your intervention, the Hawker did unwittingly reveal that he gets his goods from the ships in the dock and no doubt illegally"* Blackthorn stated.

Whilst he did not have the time or manpower to investigate all of the goings on at the Harbour, at least they now establishing that there are underhanded dealings going on with HMS Bengal where the Captain was murdered, Blackthorn pondered.

"*Well done, Arun,*" Blackthorn said with a clap on Aruns shoulders. Arun felt a warmth of pride surging through his body from Blackthorn's words and simply said, "*thank you.*" Blackthorn knew that even being a Scotland Yard Inspector was enough to unlock the mouths of these people, but Arun was proving useful and resourceful. Whilst he would have to find alternative sources of information, particularly through his network of informers, he realised that Arun could prove especially useful in gleaning information from those who would not readily speak with him.

Apart from the encounter with the Hawker where Arun had skilfully prised out some information, every other face and every shadow they engaged with seemed to frustratingly hold and protect the city's secret stories and hidden life.

Blackthorn, sensing the weight of their fruitless morning, decided a break was in order. "*Ever tried the classic pie and mash, Arun?*" Blackthorn's voice held a jovial lilt, his attempt to lighten the mood. The friendly slap on Arun's back, though well-intentioned, made him flinch. Hesitating briefly, Arun nodded, "*Okay, Sir.* "*No need to call me Sir lad, just call me Blackthorn, all my friends he said with a smile*" Arun stared at Blackthorn wondering whether he had a first name, but not wishing to pry, he merely nodded and sad "*okay Blackthorn.*"

Before long, Blackthorn and Arun found themselves standing before the welcoming allure of a lively tavern. The entrance promised warmth and respite, and as they stepped inside, the vibrant atmosphere enveloped them. Sturdy oak beams arched overhead, bearing the weight of many jovial moments. They absorbed the rich symphony of hearty laughter, the melodic clinking of glasses, and the animated hum of myriad conversations that filled the room.

The air within the tavern was thick and intoxicating, a robust blend of the sweet, sharp scent of ale, the smoky whispers of burning tobacco, and the comforting embrace of warmth emanating from a grand, crackling fireplace. A whimsical touch adorned the space above the busy bar—a carved wooden mermaid, poised with timeless grace. Her ethereal beauty played a stark contrast against the rugged authenticity of an aged set of medieval armour placed beside her, telling silent tales of valour and battles long past.

The innkeeper, a robust man with a voice that resonated with the warmth of hospitality, cut through the tapestry of ambient sounds. "*Inspector Blackthorn! Always an honour!*" His voice boomed with genuine pleasure as he gestured toward a waiting table. The patrons, sensing the arrival of authority, vacated the spot with a mix of hurried respect and subtle apprehension.

As they made their way through the crowded space, a subtle shift in the room's energy became perceptible. The lively chaos seemed to simmer down to a gentle murmur, eyes turning curiously toward Arun, whose exotic appearance whispered tales of distant lands. Arun, feeling the brush of numerous gazes, maintained his composure, keeping his eyes firmly ahead, navigating through the undercurrents of curiosity and the unspoken questions that filled the room.

As they settled into the warm embrace of the tavern and began perusing the menu, Blackthorn initially suggested an old favourite: steak and kidney pie. However, a delicate hiccup surfaced in the form of Arun's religious dietary restrictions. Arun, feeling a blend of unease and respect, gently interrupted the order. His voice carried a soft trepidation as he shared a piece of his cultural essence, explaining that his Hindu beliefs precluded him from consuming beef. He spoke with a subtle vulnerability, allowing a glimpse into his revered traditions and the spiritual convictions that guided his choices.

Blackthorn, momentarily caught in the crosswinds of surprise and contemplation, took a brief pause to process the information. His mind carefully turned the pages of understanding, seeking to respect and honour Arun's heartfelt disclosure. Moments later, his face unfurled into a warm, amicable grin, lightening the atmosphere with the soft glow of camaraderie and acceptance.

"Well, it seems like the pie is all mine today!" he joked, allowing humour to bridge the gaps between their diverse worlds. His response, sprightly and considerate, revealed a level of cultural sensitivity quite remarkable for the Victorian era. His words danced with a graceful acceptance, respecting the boundaries of Arun's faith with a light-hearted touch.

"Would bread, broth and cheese be a comfortable choice for you, then?" Blackthorn asked, his tone carrying a soft echo of hospitality and a willingness to adapt, ensuring that Arun felt valued and respected in the shared space of their unique camaraderie.

In the warm, dimly lit corners of the tavern, Blackthorn and Arun found solace in a brief respite, their table laden with modest offerings that echoed the rustic charm of their surroundings. The air around them was thick with the residue of unsaid words and the shadowy whispers of the morning's trials. They dined in a silence that spoke volumes, each man entangled in the murky web of thoughts, sifting through the frustrations and dead ends that had marked their journey thus far.

In the quietude, the clinking of utensils and the subdued symphony of surrounding conversations became the subtle soundtrack to their contemplation. They were on a precipice, looking ahead at a labyrinthine path shrouded in mystery and intrigue. Every morsel, every sip was accompanied by the weight of the challenge that lay ahead, their minds fervently racing to connect the dots, to uncover the veiled truths that lingered in the shadows of the city's underworld.

A sudden shift broke the silence, the resonant timbre of Blackthorn's voice cutting through the ambient noise, carving spaces of clarity in the fog of uncertainty. "*Arun,*" he began, each word carrying the strength of purpose, "*I will delve back into the cryptic alleys, confront the grim faces and clandestine figures that lurk in the city's hidden crevices.*" He laid out the plan with a strategist's precision, "*You should seek out information from your fellow* lascars, *see what truths or whispers you can glean from them.*"

The fabric of their strategy solidified in the quiet agreement that followed, a mutual understanding weaving through the spaces between spoken words. Blackthorn, embodying the spirit of unwavering determination, rose from his seat. His hand left a subtle glitter of coins on the table, an unspoken gratitude for the brief sanctuary they had found within the tavern's embracing walls.

"*Time is a swift current, lad,*" Blackthorn's words echoed with urgency. "*We are in pursuit of a cunning murderer.*" His eyes flickered with the flame of resolution, kindling the spaces of doubt with sparks of hope and determination.

I will meet you back at the HMS Bengal in three hours, where I will want to hear what you have discovered and speak with the First Mate and Mr Khan. With that, Blackthorn turned on his heels and headed off, giving off all the confident manner of a man on a mission.

CHAPTER 8: DUPLICITY

At the shadowy corner of the dock where the HMS Bengal loomed ominously, Khan skulked away from the ship, moving as silently as a ghost, his every step filled with dread. He was acutely aware of the eyes that could be watching him from the deck above, and the pounding of his heart matched the ticking of the time bomb he carried within him. Gone were the trappings of his identity as a Lascar overseer and sailor, instead, he wore civilian clothes, a disguise as thin as a spider's web. As he descended the ramp, his once-imposing figure now appeared as though carved from granite, his tense muscles coiled like a spring. Swiftly, he vanished into the chaotic swarm of laborers on the docks, a lone wolf among the sheep.

At the docks' entrance, a tall, cadaverous man with a serious face and sharp attire awaited Khan. Dressed in a sleek waistcoat and top hat, he was clearly not from the working classes as he exuded an air of aristocracy and privilege. The two men exchanged a brief, furtive greeting before slipping into a hansom cab that would transport them into the heart of London's shadows.

Inside the confined space of the cab, the tall man turned to Khan, his eyes drilling into him with a ferocity that alerted Khan's keen senses. "*So, the Captain is dead, but not according to plan,*" he hissed, his words dripping with venom, more an accusation than a question.

Khan turned to meet his piercing gaze, "*Mr. Parkinson, rest assured, all is going as planned,*" Khan replied tersely, his voice laden with a slight tone of tension.

"*Proceeding as planned?*" Parkinson spat back, his tone incensed, his anger palpable. "*Why in God's name was Sir Reginald brutally murdered instead of a tidy accident as we'd discussed?*"

Khan's heart raced, but his exterior betrayed no hint of panic. He was a man who had clawed his way up the ranks through brute force, determination, and unyielding submission to his white superiors. "*Sir,*" he began, his voice hushed, "*there were unforeseen complications, and the plan had to adapt. I cannot reveal more at this stage, but rest assured, we have it under control, except for one matter...*" Khan tailed off in his response.

"*What matter?*" Parkinson demanded, his voice sharp and strident.

"*Sir, please, keep clam,*" Khan implored, knowing that he had no desire to have this conversation and that time was of the essence.

"*Mind your manners when you are speaking with me,*" Parkinson retorted. "*You need me to complete this enterprise*" he said trying to calm himself. "*Now what's the bloody problem?*" Parkinson asked with annoyance.

Khan, taking a deep breath, explained that that the discovery of Sir Reginald and the bloody knife was planned, and an immediate suspect set up in the form of Arun Varma. He went on to explain to Parkinson that the plan was working until the arrival of Inspector Blackthorn from Scotland Yard, whom for whatever reason took to Arun and indeed, ended up securing the services of Arun as his assistant on this case.

Parkinson stared at Khan in disbelief. "What?" he exclaimed, aghast. "Are you telling me that this Lascar is now aiding a Scotland Yard Inspector in hunting the real murderer?"

Khan nodded, his face devoid of emotion, as if reciting an irrevocable truth. "Yes," he affirmed. "But fear not, I have measures in place to ensure that the Inspector and Arun do not uncover too much in their investigations", Khan said with a vicious smile that oozed venom.

"*I don't want to know*" said Parkinson, with a hint of fear in his voice. "I *have no part in any violence, my role is simply as a facilitator*" Parkinson said nervously.

Khan glared at Parkinson, piercing him with a look of pure malice. "*Oh no Sir, you are very much part of this venture, and don't you ever forget that*" Khan said in a menacing voice that Parkinson could not misinterpret it other than as a threat.

Parkinson swallowed hard, all his previous air of superiority and confidence vanishing under the weight of Khan's glare and words. Khan sensing this pressed his point home. "*I may call upon you again, but until you hear from me, it would be wise for you to keep your mouth closed*" he hissed.

"*Now, if you would kindly stop here, I will get on with my tasks,*" Khan said, his tone now less subservient. Parkinson urged the driver to stop and allowed Khan to get off. He watched as Khan disappeared amongst the throng of the crowds and the thick fog, suddenly feeling very frightened.

Khan navigated the teeming thoroughfares, oblivious to onlookers and sidestepping panhandlers, making his way to Cheapside—London's epicentre of affluence. This bustling avenue stood as the city's financial pulse, not just a marketplace but a showcase of conspicuous prosperity. Amid the cacophony of horse-drawn carriages and hawkers' shouts, the affluent and the rural visitors jostled for space. A tapestry of aromas enveloped the air: the smoky sweetness of chestnuts, the yeasty promise of bakery loaves, mingled with the musk of horseflesh and the sharpness of metalwork from goldsmiths at their forges.

Through the parade of luxurious mercer and goldsmith displays, Khan slipped into a narrow side street. He glanced over his shoulder for any followers before entering the goldsmith's backyard, which led to a cluster of dilapidated dwellings housing the laborers. He rapped thrice at a door, paused, then knocked once more. A hulking figure soon opened it, admitting Khan into a dim, musty space redolent with the odour of mildew and human neglect. The room, simply furnished with a pair of beds, a table with chairs, and a bubbling pot over the fire, was home to another stout man with broad muscular shoulders, whose silhouette blended with the room's dim candlelight, appearing to lack a neck.

Rising to meet Khan, he offered a firm handshake, followed by the other occupant. Seated together, they leaned in for a hushed conversation.

Khan addressed them with a frosty tone, *"Mr. Topley, Mr. Styles, continue monitoring Arun Verma and observe the Bengal's traffic."* They acknowledged with silent nods.

"One last point," Khan added, his voice hardening. *"Also, watch Mr. Parkinson. Report any odd encounters or actions. He is not to be trusted; the man's a coward,"* he finished with a disdainful curl of the lip.

Standing to leave, Khan locked eyes with Topley and Styles, his gaze sharp. *"Remember, your generous pay, demands unwavering vigilance and necessary action."*

Topley, his features straining against his collar, assured Khan with an eager tone, *"rest assured, our reputation is second to none,"* his affirmation culminating in a malicious grin.

CHAPTER 8: UNENVIABLE TASK

As Arun watched Blackthorn stride away to visit his network of informers and to comb the crime ridden back streets, Arun suddenly felt a chill run through him, not from the bitter easterly winds, but from Blackthorns words which echoed in his ears, "*You should seek out information from your fellow* lascars, *see what truths or whispers you can glean from them. We are in pursuit of a cunning murderer.*"

Arun tried to compose himself and sought assistance from the bare whisper of strength he felt in his body as he set off for the Dockside and the return to the HMS Bengal. He felt his stomach knot up with anxiety at the thought of boarding the ship, wondering how the crew and his friends would greet him. Would he still be seen as the main suspect for the murder of Sir Reginald or someone who was seemly escaping justice by becoming a pawn for the Inspector. Arun wondered how his close friend and confidant Akash would respond to his return and the questions that he must ask him and others.

As Arun made his way through the thronging mass of people, trying to ignore the discriminating glances and occasional insults hurled at him, he reflected on his journey to where he found himself now. It was vastly different from his quiet, but happy life back in India, surrounded by a loving family, close friends and the glow he felt every time he saw Priya. Arun's heart ached to be back in those carefree days, to feel the warm sun on his back, but despite this, he knew deep down that he was not the same person. The sudden death of his father had changed everything. Tearing down the walls of his dreams, the poetry that coursed through his veins was just a distant memory now. A wave of despair and melancholy was starting to take hold of him as clouds grew dark and freezing rain came pouring down.

Arun wrapped his all to thin coat around him and took in a deep breath, wiping the tears that intermingled with the rain, he beseeched his mind to return to the tasks at hand and to give him purpose. As Arun quickened his pace in the vain attempt to beat the rain, he was roughly pushed aside by a man he had not seen.

The man vanished into the crowd, but he was convinced that he heard the man say, *"keep your mouth shut coolie or you will never speak again."*

Arun's eyes darted around in panic, seeking the figure who had jostled him. Peering through the curtain of relentless rain and the dimming light, he thought he caught a glimpse of two stocky figures near a vendor's stand, one with a pipe, giving him a taunting smirk. He brushed the raindrops from his face for a clearer view, only to find they had vanished. Over and over, Arun replayed the encounter in his head, seeking the reality of that brief contact. An internal shiver spreading through him, he attempted to reassure himself, hoping the voice and the shove were just tricks of his anxious mind, a mere accident.

Yet, amidst the whirl of his thoughts, a persistent inner whisper cautioned him, "Be cautious, my son."

A little while later, Arun stood in front of the imposing hulk of HMS Bengal. The heavy rain had driven many of the men below deck and there seemed to be little activity. He ran up the ramp to board the ship and was immediately confronted by the First Mate, Chief Middleton.

He fixed Arun with an unwelcoming stare and stood as though to block his way *"So has your brown arse been sent back to us then"* he growled sarcastically.

Arun tried not to show his fear and with an attempt to appear calm said, *"Inspector Blackthorn has asked me to return to the ship Sir."*

"What? To spy on us? You his lacky now, are you, boy?" scowled Middleton.

"No sir" Arun said, *"he will be coming to visit you in a few hours and asked me to meet him here."* Arun said, trying his best to hide his true reason for returning to the ship.

Middleton fixed Arun with a piercing look, trying to decipher what he had just been told and to work out whether Arun was lying. After what seemed an eternity of silence and growing tension, Middleton responded. *"Make sure you stay to your quarters boy and don't let me catch you wandering around the ship, particularly where the officers are,"* he said in a stern and uncompromising tone.

Arun nodded and said, *"yes Sir."*

As Arun made to move towards the lower decks of the ship, Middleton laid a hand on his shoulders, roughly turning him around. "One last thing." He growled menacingly.

"You are still under my command and if you fuck with me, it will be more than a lashing you will receive. Do I make myself clear!" he roared in Arun's face.

Arun felt his bowels lurch as panic gripped him. The rain lashing on his face helped him mask his fear and with significant effort, he replied, *"yes Sir, I understand and mean you no harm."*

Middleton looked at him, grunted something under his breath and walked off. Arun let out a huge sigh of relief and headed to the lower decks.

Meanwhile, in the dim, dank corners where shadows whispered the sinister sagas of the city, Blackthorn embarked on a merciless mission of revelation. Inspector Blackthorn spent time visiting the hovels where his informants or 'snouts' as he called them lived and worked. The icy rain made his task more miserable, but he was determined to find out as much as possible about HMS Bengal and its crew. His snouts knew everything that took place in the underbelly of this city, particularly around the docks, which were the main source of illicit goods. They were privy to the whispers of crime and its perpetrators and for a price and promise of anonymity, they would reveal all.

Blackthorn cornered his best snout, a wiry man with the deep marks of smallpox on his face and yellow nicotine-stained teeth, "hey paddy, how are you?" Blackthorn said in a friendly manner.

Paddy screwed his face in a twisted grin, the large gaps between his teeth, giving his face a ghoulish look. *"Hello guv"* he rasped. *"What are you wanting today?* he asked Blackthorn.

Blackthorn, his face looking serious said, *"listen Paddy, I need to know everything you know about HMS Bengal, its crew and those that deal with the ship locally. This is important and part of a murder case, so do not mess me around."* He said pointedly to Paddy, whom he knew would draw out a conversation to get more coin from Blackthorn.

Paddy took in a deep breath and stared at Blackthorn, *"what's in it for me Guv"* he enquired off Blackthorn.

"The usual Paddy," Blackthorn said in an impatient tone, *"and I am short on time, so make it good and I might add a little extra for your cooperation"* he added.

Paddy smiled, although to Blackthorn, it always looked like a grimace. *"You know I always like to help the law Mr Blackthorn, so I will share all I know from the little birds on the street,"* he said with a conspiratorial smile.

Arun found himself amidst a quiet corner of the ship, sharing a moment of secrecy with Akash, his most trusted companion aboard. Just freed from a gruelling shift and slipping into their mother tongue, Akash extended a warm welcome, his eyes gleaming with eager curiosity.

"*So, you're back,*" he exclaimed, breath heavy with anticipation, ready to soak in the sagas of Arun's experiences. "*How are you holding up? What unfolded?*" Akash inquired, concealing his underlying angst beneath a façade of usual cheerfulness.

Arun sensed an unspoken tension lurking beneath Akash's jovial surface. "*It's been chaotic, brother. The turn of events has not given me a moment of peace,*" Arun confessed, his voice tinged with exhaustion. "*My sole aim is to vindicate myself and aid Inspector Blackthorn in uncovering the truth behind Sir Reginald's murder*".

Akash's gaze drifted away, lost in a blend of empathy and sorrow. "*I feel your turmoil. I have been vocal in defending your innocence, reassuring others of your incapacity to commit such a cruel act,*" he said, managing a strained smile. "*Beware of Khan, Arun. He thirsts for your downfall, desiring nothing but to see you hang,*" he added solemnly.

"*Khan is but a merciless barbarian, deriving joy from the agony of others,*" Arun retaliated, a defiant tone resonating in his voice, eager to steer the conversation away from the prevailing gloom and peril.

"Akash, I find myself in desperate need of your assistance," Arun confessed, his face shrouded in seriousness. "*Do you know anything that might shed light on what happened to Sir Reginald and what is happening now on the ship?* He enquired.

Akash took a long pause, his face a contortion of fear and anxiety, "*what did you want to know*" he asked Arun nervously.

"*Have you heard anything about the theft of documents from the Captains quarters or any whispers among the crew that can shed light on what happened*" Arun replied with an imploring look at Akash. A silence engulfed them as Akash grappled with an internal turmoil, appearing to juggle between the revelations he should unveil and the dangers that loomed in speaking.

Resolved to stand by his friend, Akash composing himself, sat upright and turned to Arun, his voice barely a whisper. *"I have heard rumours that there was bad blood between Sir Reginald and Middleton"* Akash began. *"The gossip was that Middleton wanted command of the ship and felt that Sir Reginald was hindering his progression."*

Arun remained quiet, taking in what Akash was saying, but allowing the man time and space to continue. *"I haven't seen it first hand, as you know we are no more than lackeys, but others have heard the junior officers speak about this, but that's all I know on this rumour"* Akash said quietly. Arun pondered the information shared by Akash, but decided not to comment upon it, rather he will convey this to Blackthorn and let him draw his own conclusions.

Akash, lost in his own thoughts, was gently jolted out of his revery by Arun, who asked him, *"do you know anything else that might help in me clearing my name"* Arun said, purposely focusing Akash on his plight to avoid being seen as Inspector Blackthorns assistant in an investigation.

Akash, after a long pause, looked earnestly at Arun, *"I have heard that Khan is in deep debt from his gambling and is under pressure to pay back money. I do not know how much he owes, but it must be bad if he is asking some of the other lascars for a loan, knowing they earn a pittance"* Akash said with a smile.

"Has he ever asked you for money," Arun asked Akash. *"Yes, once or twice, but I told him that I have barely enough money to support myself"* Akash said with a melancholy look.

Arun considered all that Akash had told him and knew that it was significant, and he could not wait to tell Blackthorn.

Akash suddenly rose to his feet, mentioning he needed to get back to his responsibilities to avoid severe punishment. Arun said his farewells, expressing gratitude for his assistance. Watching Akash walk away left Arun with a lingering suspicion that something significant was being concealed, sensing a noticeable anxiety in the man. Arun found himself uncertain, questioning whether the heavy, tense environment onboard was clouding his perceptions, or if the mystery surrounding Sir Reginald's murder was indeed deeper and more complicated than he initially thought. He decided he would try and speak to the other *lascars* he trusted to see if he could learn anything else.

Akash, consumed by a tumult of emotions, ascended to the upper deck to resume his arduous tasks. As he navigated through the ship, he was abruptly seized by Khan's menacing presence.

Khan, wearing a grimace, clutched Akash violently from behind, forcing him against the ship's rugged wall. *"Speaking carelessly again, are you?"* Khan interrogated, his face marred with a cruel sneer *"I know you and that bastard Arun are thick as thieves and been huddled in a corner whispering like a couple of girls"* Khan said to Akash, his muscled hands reaching up for his throat.

Akash feeling a wave of terror sweep across him, struggled to find words. He looked at Khan with a pleading look and gasped, *"no sir, I have not told Arun anything that he doesn't know already,"* *"I was simply enquiring about how he was faring given the suspicions of murder that circle him"* Akash said trying to calm Khan's evident fury.

Khan's grip on Akash's throat tightened as his eyes pierced into him. *"Don't you lie to me, you worthless piece of shit"* Khan growled. *"Don't you forget that if it weren't for me, you would be doing the hardest time possible on this ship and on half rations"* he hissed at Akash, moving his face closer to Akash to emphasise his words.

Akash recoiled, writhing under the oppression of Khan's grasp, his senses assailed by the stench of alcohol and stale tobacco. Desperate pleas escaped Akash's lips in ragged breaths, begging for reprieve. Through spluttering breaths Akash begged Khan to release his hold. *"Please sir"* he said repeatedly.

Khan, conscious of being seen by others, released his hold on Akash, but continued to stare coldly at him. *"Don't forget your involvement in this"* Khan spat at Akash.

Akash, taking deep breaths to recover, said in a hoarse voice, *"I have thought of nothing but my role in this drama since the Murder and am ashamed of what I have done."*

Khan's expression grew darker, and he pulled out a vicious looking knife, pointing it malevolently close to Akash's eyes." *Hear my words boy, if you want to live, keep your mouth shut!"* he said with a cold calmness which seemed more frightening to Akash than his wrath.

Akash nodded pitifully, *"I will not say a word"* he said with a tone that did not carry conviction.

Khan stared at him, trying to read Akash's thoughts, said, *"besides you will be a richer man for your help,"* trying to sound more jovial. With that, Khan tuned on his heels, departing with a menacing grace, Khan's formidable physique loomed like a titan amidst the constrained pathways of the ship's lower deck.

CHAPTER 8: SHIP OF SECRETS

Arun, fruitless from his chats with other *lascars*, who were clearly frightened to speak with him, waited for the arrival of Blackthorn by wiling away time visiting his old haunts on the ship, paying special homage to the kitchen in which he toiled to add colour and flavour to their meagre rations. Arun's reminiscences were interrupted by his old kitchen companion James, whose rounded body and face, stumbled into the kitchen galley, knocking over some pans.

"Aye aye, I heard you were back onboard," James said with a warm smile. *"How are you, Laddie?"* James said with a quizzical look at Arun.

Arun smiled and with a weary look said, *"Well life is certainly not dull."*

James bellowed with laughter, *"I have missed your humour!* he exclaimed.

Arun was warmed by the greeting and exchange with James and said with a serious look, *"Are you not worried to be seen with me?"*

"Fuck the others Laddie, they don't frighten me," James retorted, *"I know you didn't kill the Captain Laddie, there are other buggers on board who are ahead of you for that cowardly crime,"* he said.

Arun looked at James for a while and with a tinge of excitement rising inside him, asked, *"Do you know who did it then, James?"*

James, looking serious and a little pensive, lowered his voice and said, *"No Laddie, I don't know for sure, but I have my suspicions."*

Arun trying to control his frustration at James's vague reply, asked, *"Who do you suspect?"*

James stared at Arun for some time, his face twisting with a myriad of thoughts. *"Put it this way,"* he said. *"If I was a gambling man, and I am, I would be looking at an officer and his sidekick,"* he said with a mischievous smile. Then his face darkening, James went on, *"I just work down here and mind my own business. I have seen nor heard anything that makes me certain about who did it."*

Arun sensed that James did not want to get involved and he knew that it would be pointless to push him any further. James stretched out his hands to shake Arun's and with that he said, *"Best be on my way. Middleton is in a foul mood and looking to thrash someone."*

Arun took James's hands and wished him well and said goodbye. Arun was all alone in the kitchen again and was left to ponder what James had told him. Although James was being cryptic, Arun felt that there was a clue to the murder in what he said and vowed to add this to the information he would share with Inspector Blackthorn.

Arun, realising the time, decided to move up toward the main deck to wait for Blackthorn. As he made his way through the mass of bodies toiling in the lower decks and avoiding all manner of goods and equipment hurried to reach the top deck and to rid his lungs of the heavy odours of the lower decks. To his dismay he found the menacing form of Khan waiting at the steps to the top deck.

Khan glaring at Arun said with a sarcastic bow, *"Well if it isn't Lord Arun."*

Arun froze and looked around to see if there were any other sailors around him, but they all had vanished. He took in a deep breath to calm his nerves and said, *"Mr Khan, what can I do for you?"*

"Always the gentlemen, eh boy" Khan scowled at Arun.

Arun did not respond; he knew that Khan was looking for any excuse to cause him harm. His silence irritated Khan and with his voice rising said, *"I know you have been whispering into the ears of the other bastard lascars. It is not wise to try and step into the shoes of others to learn things you do not need to know,"* he said cryptically, his hands stroking the dagger hanging by his waist.

Sensing the rising tension in the air, Arun knew he had to get to the top deck and away from Khan. *"Inspector Blackthorn will be waiting for me on the top deck, Mr Khan,"* Arun said in a voice that struggled to remain calm.

Khan glared at Arun, every sinew of his body visibly throbbing to do him harm. Arun braced for blows from Khan; they never came. Khan continued to glare at Arun, his mind battling his next move. After what seemed an eternity, Khan moved closer to Arun and whispered in a chilling voice, *"I am not finished with you, boy."* With that he turned and walked off.

Arun drew in a deep breath and let out a groan in relief. He then scrambled up the steps into the top deck of the ship, letting the fresh air calm his nerves.

Arun felt a wash of relief as he noticed the approaching figure of Inspector Blackthorn at the Dock, making his way decisively toward the HMS Bengal with a visage marked by determination. Acknowledging Arun with a nod, Blackthorn made his confident ascent up the plank, boarding the ship. Arun attempted to approach and welcome him, but found his way obstructed by Middleton, who was covertly observing Blackthorn.

With an expression marred by frustration and fury, Middleton marched past Arun, intercepting Blackthorn with barely a veil of civility in his voice. *"Inspector Blackthorn,"* Middleton greeted with scant warmth.

Blackthorn, unfazed, greeted him, *"Ahh Chief, just the man I wanted to see."*

Arun standing nearby, did not move towards Blackthorn but decided to observe the exchange.

"What can I do for you Inspector? This is a working vessel," Middleton said dryly.

Blackthorn ignored the barbed comment, *"This is a murder enquiry Chief, and I am under duty to investigate it. This ship is a central part of the case,"* Blackthorn said in a matter-of-fact tone.

Middleton, clearly annoyed at Blackthorns response, simply said, *"So what is it you want?"*

"I would like to speak with you and Mr Khan and anyone else serving on this ship that maybe of interest to me," Blackthorn replied in a commanding tone.

Middleton eyed Blackthorn with suspicion but knew he could not stand in the way of Scotland Yard.

"Can I meet you in your quarters in 30 mins?" Blackthorn asked Middleton.

Middleton was a little surprised by the question. *"You don't want to speak now?"* Middleton asked in a confused tone.

"No, I need to see Arun first to ensure he is okay," Blackthorn said.

Middleton screwed his eyes in an attempt to read Blackthorn's mind. *"He is fine, I will meet you in 30mins."* Middleton said and with that he turned with an intention to walk off.

"One moment Chief," Blackthorn said. *"While I am speaking with you and Khan, I would like Arun to return to portside and wait for me there."* Middleton looked at Blackthorn, shrugged his shoulders in acknowledgment and walked off.

Blackthorn approached Arun who was still digesting the exchange between Middleton and Blackthorn and working out why Blackthorn wanted him to wait at the dockside.

"So how did you get on," Blackthorn said in a quiet voice, urging Arun to move to a quiet part of the deck and away from prying

eyes.

Arun composed the whirling thoughts in his head and began. *"Well, I have discovered a tangle of webs that may hold the secret to this puzzle,"* he began.

Blackthorn looked at him with a mix of curiosity and mild scepticism. *"Go on then,"* he said.

Arun proceeded to brief Blackthorn about his conversations with Akash and then with Middleton and, finally his encounter with Khan. He felt as though his words tumbled out of him without context or any articulation. Blackthorn stared at Arun whilst considering all that he had been told, unpicking the embers of truth and clues from the tales.

Arun waited for Blackthorn to respond, feeling a wave of doubt and insecurity at what he had relayed and its import to the case.

Blackthorn let out a deep breath and said, *"Arun if what you have told me is true, then we are indeed making progress. It is clear that the murder of Sir Reginald holds beneath it a web of conspiracy that is more complex than we had imagined."*

Arun felt a surge of excitement and pride at this response, his senses alert to the consequences of what he had discovered. Blackthorn deep in thought and reflection went on to share that what Arun had said echoed with what he had discovered through his snouts. There was criminality and shady dealings associated with the ship, whether it be the illicit sale of goods that came off the ship or the machinations of those that ran the ship. It had a reputation for being a vessel for corruption and crime.

Arun considered what Blackthorn had shared and his pulse quickened at the consequences of what he had heard. *"Do you think that the culprits of the murder of Sir Reginald are on board this ship?"* he asked Blackthorn.

Blackthorn looked at Arun with an intensity that made Arun

flinch. *"Yes, I think the answer lies somewhere in the deep recesses of this ship and those that command it"* he said. *"The task now is to unravel this mystery from the inside. Let me speak with Chief Middleton, Khan and some of the crew and see if I can piece together the evidence that will hold those responsible to justice"* he said with a determined look.

"I want you to wait for me at the Old Sea Dog tavern at the end of this dock whilst I speak to Middleton and Khan," said Blackthorn.

Arun felt strangely disappointed by the suggestion. *"Why? I can be of assistance"* he said to Blackthorn.

"No! You will only risk your safety by doing so" Blackthorn retorted.

Arun, despite his urge to postulate, sensed that it was futile to argue with Blackthorn and acquiesced to his command. *"Okay, I will wait for you at the Ships Mate Tavern,"* Arun said reluctantly.

"Good," said Blackthorn. *"I will meet you there in an hour or so. Here are a few pennies for you to buy yourself a drink,"* he added with a smile, before walking off to see Middleton.

Blackthorn found Middleton in his chamber. He knocked on the door and was let in by a voice that was far from friendly. *"So, how can I help you Inspector?"* Middleton said in a cold tone, whilst inviting Blackthorn to sit down.

"I would like to know everything you can tell me about your relationship with Sir Reginald and any light you can shed on why he was murdered," said Blackthorn in a tone that brooked no dissembling from Middleton.

Middleton cautioned himself to be professional and to the point. He began to tell Blackthorn about his 10 years as First Officer to Sir Reginald and painted a picture of himself as that of a loyal leftenant, unwavering in his support to Sir Reginald.

Blackthorn stood up and paced the cabin whilst considering the response from Middleton. Middleton shifted uneasily in his chair waiting for a response from Blackthorn.

Blackthorn looked at Middleton, his eyes boring into him as though he was disentangling the words that were spoken to find the hidden meanings. *"So, in your words, you never had a disagreeable word with Sir Reginald?"* Blackthorn asked, his voice a quiver of questioning disbelief.

"I didn't say that Inspector," Middleton said abruptly. You cannot manage a ship without disagreement. *"What I said was that I respected Sir Reginald, and we had a cordial and professional relationship."*

Blackthorn, seemingly ignoring the statement from Middleton, switched tack, *"Do you know anyone who would want to harm or kill Sir Reginald?"* he asked with a fierce gaze at Middleton.

Middleton felt uneasy at the line of questioning but composed himself. *"Unless you have something direct to ask me Inspector, my answer remains the same. I had exceptionally good working relations with Sir Reginald, and I am not aware of anyone who would want to do harm to Sir Reginald."*

Blackthorn, intuitively feeling a sense of dishonesty from Middleton, subtly altered his approach. *"Have you ever felt a wave of frustration or anger because your path to further career advancement seemed obstructed by Sir Reginald?"* he queried.

Middleton, caught off guard by the question, paused to regain his composure. *"Blocked? What do you mean?"* he retorted sharply.

A faint smile graced the corners of Blackthorn's mouth, sensing that he had touched a vulnerable spot in Middleton. He deliberately delayed his response, allowing a heavy silence to amplify the tension within the cabin. *"Middleton, you understand precisely what I'm implying,"* he replied icily. *"Isn't it quite natural that after a decade as a First Mate, there would be a fervent aspiration to assume command of the ship?"* he probed further.

Middleton, his face growing puce with anger and concern, glared at Blackthorn and then straightening his back replied, *"I know you are trying to trap me into admitting that I had some reason to murder Sir Reginald, but that's not how it works in the navy.,"* Without drawing a breath, he continued. *"If you had any idea what it is like to be a sailor, you would know that we are used to the order of things when it comes to command and there was no dishonour in serving under a man like Sir Reginald."*

Blackthorn sensing that his conversation was likely to go around in circles, paused, looking at Middleton and then, choosing his words carefully, said. *"I wish to converse with some of your other officers, specifically Kabir Khan. Any objections?"* he asked, his tone more of a courteous formality than a genuine request for consent.

Middleton, embodying the demeanour of a volcano on the verge of eruption, tersely responded, *"No objections, Inspector."*

Blackthorn gave a nod of acknowledgment. As he prepared to exit, he pivoted towards Middleton, inquiring further, *"What is the nature of your association with Kabir Khan?"*

Caught off guard, Middleton's head snapped up, and a momentary pause filled the room as he gathered his thoughts for a response. *"Khan serves as the* ghat sarang *on this vessel, Inspector. He assists in managing the natives onboard, who tend to be inherently idle,"* he said, a demeaning smile subtly crossing his face.

Blackthorn, sensing Middleton's evasiveness, pushed further. *"Do your interactions with Khan extend beyond professional boundaries aboard the ship?"* he asked, concealing his scepticism towards Middleton's explanation.

Middleton replied defensively, *"What need would I have to have any dealings with Khan outside of his and my duties?* Middleton retorted. *"Khan might be the overseer of the lascars, but he is one himself and I don't need a lap dog like you do Inspector,"* Middleton added with an obvious reference to Blackthorn and Arun.

Blackthorn was unmoved by Middleton's ranting responses. *"The murder of Sir Reginald did not happen at the hands of a malevolent spirit, but at the hands of one or more of this crew,"* Blackthorn said whilst gazing coldly at Middleton. *"I will get to the bottom of this."* And with that Blackthorn turned on his heels and left Middleton.

For the next thirty minutes, Blackthorn engaged in conversations with various officers, probing the workings of the ship, its undisclosed facts, and the circumstances surrounding the location where Sir Reginald's life was tragically taken. The officers' answers echoed in similarity, a practiced uniformity, suggesting a prior briefing and alignment on responses. Despite the stifling repetition, Blackthorn's frustration was tempered with a lack of surprise at the apparent rehearsed responses he received.

Blackthorn went in search of Khan. He found him sitting with his two of his *tindals*, deep in conversation.

They looked up in unison as Blackthorn approached them. With a subtle shake of his head, Khan told the *tindals* to leave. Khan stood up, his towering body, face framed with a long beard and deep black eyes bored into Blackthorn as he approached. *"How can I help you Inspector?"* he said with an even tone.

Blackthorn looking at Khan, suddenly felt pity for the *lascars* who had to work and live under this man. *"I understand from Chief Middleton that you are a most important man on this ship, Mr Khan and there is no one who knows the inner working of this ship better than you,"* Blackthorn replied, not exactly being faithful in what Middleton had told him about Khan.

Khan, narrowing his eyes, replied, *"That is kind of Chief Middleton to say, but I am just a humble and loyal servant of this ship,"* attempting to sound humble.

Blackthorn smiled and, clapping Khan on his shoulders, said, *"You are too modest Mr Khan, I have heard that without you, this ship would not function properly."*

Khan looked at Blackthorn trying to work out what Blackthorn was trying to do.

"May I sit?" Blackthorn asked.

Khan nodded and invited him to sit on the heavy sacks next to him.

"What do you know about the murder of Sir Reginald?" Blackthorn asked, deciding to cut to the chase rather than continue with pleasantries.

Khan was expecting the question and calmy responded, *"Arun is the man you should be arresting for the murder of Sir Reginald. His kitchen knife was found next to Sir Reginald's body and that boy was always wandering the ship looking into places he had no right to be in."*

Blackthorn looked at Khan and with a hint of a smile said, *"I do not believe it was Mr Verma, but I am interested to see how much you wish him to be arrested as the culprit. Why is that?"* Blackthorn asked quizzically.

Khan clearly annoyed at Blackthorn's question and with a shrug of his shoulders, looked Blackthorn in the eyes and said in a voice dripping with venom, *"It is not only I who thinks Arun is guilty Inspector and once you have finished with him, the Navy will have its own way of meting out justice."*

"May I remind you that the HMS Bengal is docked in London and therefore this case falls under the jurisdiction of Scotland Yard. We will determine who is guilty or not." Blackthorn rasped, trying to hide his annoyance at Khan's lack of cooperation and attempts to deflect all attention upon Arun. *"Now, I will ask some straightforward questions and I want honest answers from you Mr Khan,"* Blackthorn's voice was hard and official.

Khan sensing the growing irritation from Blackthorn changed his demeanour to one of subservience and acquiescence. *"Of course, Inspector, I am here to help in any way that I can,"* Khan said in softer tone.

Blackthorne, ignoring the obvious false tone of cooperation from Khan, pushed on. *"Apart from Mr Verma, who else had a reason to murder Sir Reginald,"* he asked.

Khan, giving an air of a man considering the question, responded, *"I honestly don't know Inspector, Sir Reginald was a well-respected man by all onboard this ship."*

Blackthorn switching tactic, asked, *"What was your relationship with Sir Reginald?"*

Khan smiled and said, *"As I said, I am but a humble servant, Inspector. My relationship with Sir Reginald was one of servant and Master. I obeyed all commands given by Sir Reginald."*

Blackthorn believed that Khan was speaking the truth in terms of how he would have acted outwardly towards Sir Reginald. This man was clearly intelligent and cunning in equal measure and would no doubt have played distinct roles with different people. *"So aside from Mr Verma, are you telling me that you can't think of anyone else who may have wanted to harm Sir Reginald?"*

Khan nodded in reply and said in a neutral tone, *"Yes, correct Inspector."*

"So why would Mr Verma want to kill Sir Reginald?" Blackthorn continued.

Khan expression changed to one of clear annoyance at the mention of Arun's name. *"He always strides around the ship as though he was better than everyone else including the officers and spoke endlessly about how he was going to better his life,"* Khan began. *"Who knows if that did not lead him into Sir Reginald's cabin to seek out the safe where the ship's treasury was held,"* Khan said, clearly happy that he had articulated a motive for the Inspector.

"How would Mr Verma learn about the safe in Sir Reginald's cabin?" asked Blackthorn.

Khan, with a smirk, replied, *"Everyone knew Inspector, it wasn't a secret."*

"So, you knew as well did you, Khan?" Blackthorn replied.

Khan was taken aback by the question, but replied calmly, *"Yes, Inspector. I knew."*

"So, according to your theory, Mr Verma, on his own, went to the Captain's cabin to steal whatever was held in the safe and in the process killed Sir Reginald?" Blackthorn asked, barely trying to hide his incredulity.

Khan sensing that Blackthorn did not believe him, shrugged his shoulder and simply said, *"It is what I think."*

Blackthorn, clearly getting annoyed, looked at Khan and said, *"From my years of experience Mr Khan, I find it hard to believe that someone on their first voyage onboard this ship would conspire to break into the safe sitting in the Captain's cabin and, in the process, kill him. The knowledge of the safe and its contents would be known to those that have sailed many times on this ship under Sir Reginald. Someone like yourself or other officers who have served him for many years, "*he concluded.

Khan shifting uneasily on the sack that he was sat on felt a tinge of fear for the first time and struggled to find the words to respond to Blackthorn.

Blackthorn sensing this pushed on. *"I understand you like gambling, Mr Khan,"* Blackthorn began. *"Do you always win?"* he asked Khan, staring intently at him, looking for any signs that may give away is true feelings and thoughts.

Khan was now feeling distinctly uncomfortable at this line of questioning. He shied away from Blackthorns gaze and clasping his hands said, *"who told you this malicious lie?*

"Come, come, Mr Khan, we are both grown men and the vice of

gambling or drinking or whoring is common to many a sailor, would you not agree?"

Khan, struggling to keep calm, nodded and said, *"So what if I gamble now and then, it's not against any rules,"* he muttered in a defiant voice.

"But it wasn't just now and then was it, Khan?" Blackthorn began. *"You are addicted to gambling and no gambler wins all the time, in fact, quite the opposite,"* Blackthorn mused.

Khan, clearly rattled, struggled to respond.

Blackthorn taking advantage of this, went on. *"It must be a very expensive habit for you Mr Khan and one that I surmise needs regular injections of cash to clear debts, am I right?"* He asked Khan pointedly.

Khan took a deep breath, taking time to gather his thoughts before saying, *"Inspector, I don't know where you have heard all these rumours about me, but if I have done something wrong, then prove it or speak to my superior,"* he said in a voice tinged with a tone saying that he had nothing further to add.

Blackthorn smiled, got up and thanked Khan for his time. *"No doubt we will speak again Mr Khan,"* he said with a piercing look at Khan. Blackthorn did not wait for a response and strode off, suddenly feeling weary and a tad nauseous being on aboard the stinking ship.

Without another word to anyone, including Middleton who was on the top deck of the ship, Blackthorn left. Blackthorn, suddenly feeling the need for a strong drink and something to eat, went to meet Arun at the Ships Mate Tavern.

Blackthorn found Arun sitting in a corner of the Tavern looking lost in his own thoughts and nursing an empty cup of Ale, no doubt bought from the money that Blackthorn had given him.

He noticed the looks from the others in the bar as he approached Arun and with an intentionally loud voice greeted him. *"Hello there, my friend, how are you?"*

Arun as though awoken from a slumber looked at Blackthorn and wondered what as to the meaning behind the theatrical greeting. *"Inspector, it's good to see you, I have been a little concerned waiting for you."*

"Oh," said Blackthorn. *"Were you afraid that I would come back with evidence of your guilt at murdering Sir Reginald,"* he said with an affected serious look.

Arun was startled at this comment and for a moment he was filled with fear and dread at what was going to happen.

Blackthorn witnessing the obvious distress in Arun's face, felt guilty and proceeded to smile and laugh. *"I'm sorry Arun, what I said was in bad taste and I was just joking,"* he said reassuringly. *"I am in desperate need of a drink and sustenance,"* he went on.

Arun visibly relaxed and said with a sigh of relief, *"I didn't know you had such a cruel streak, Blackthorn."*

Blackthorn smiled and said, *"Let me refresh your tankard Arun and order some food. We have much to reflect upon,"* he concluded.

Over the course of the following hour, replenished by drink and food, Blackthorn and Arun shared what they had learned and its implications. Blackthorn felt that they were getting close to the truth, but Arun feared the repercussions from those that they were chasing. Something inside him kept whispering that they would face danger before they reached the heart of the truth. Arun did not share this anxiety with Blackthorn for fear of being seen as a coward. He increasingly sought the approval and respect of Blackthorn, much as he had done with his father. This feeling was both confusing and familiar for Arun.

Aruns thoughts were broken by Blackthorn. *"I know it is still a little early, but let us retire for the evening, there is not much more we can do today. A good night's sleep will aid our hunt tomorrow,"* he said with a serious look. He clapped Arun on his back and said, *"I will walk you to your digs and head home."*

With that they both rose and headed through the crowed, smoking tavern into the bitterly cold evening and headed home.

Akash, feeling troubled by the events of the day and his encounters with Arun and Khan earlier needed company to ease the tangled emotions of guilt and fear that ran through him. He sought out the other lascars who were nursing their tired bodies from the labours of the day. They sat together in the constricted cargo hold which doubled as a 'sitting room,' sharing stories as they awaited their final meal before sleep. As they talked, laughed and consoled one another, the room fell silent at the arrival of Khan. Akash, like the others, wanted to retreat into the far recesses of the deck they were in. Khan surveyed the group of lascars, his cheeks twitching as he ground his teeth whilst glaring at the group.

Then, unexpectedly, Khan demeanour softened as he said, *"Akash, my brother, I would like to have a moment with you alone to speak,"* he said with a politeness that Akash and the others have never heard.

This made Akash feel more anxious, but he had no choice but to stand up and agree to follow Khan out so they could speak.

Khan, wrapping his hands around Akash's shoulders, smiled at him as he escorted him towards the top deck of the ship. When they reached the top deck, Khan turned around to Akash and said in their native tongue, "*Akash, I am your friend, I hope you know that*" he said with a tone of sincerity that disturbed Akash, but he told himself to accept it at face value.

"*Yes, Mr Khan,*" was all that Akash could muster in response.

"*Call me Kabir, lad,*" Khan said. "*I am sorry if I scared you earlier, Akash, it was not my intention,*" he went on. "*We have much in common and I want both of us to prosper. Let us start again and I was wondering whether you have seen any of the docks or the taverns there?*" He asked Akash.

Akash, still trying to understand the change in Khan's demeanour and sudden friendliness, struggled to find the words to respond. He finally said in a soft voice, "*No, Mr Khan. I mean, Kabir. I have never visited the dockside taverns, could never afford it,*" he said with a childlike voice.

Part of him was excited at the thought of being able to experience and sample the London Taverns, but he was also wary of Khan.

Khan smiled reassuringly at Akash, "*Come let me take you out for a drink and bite to eat.*" We can speak more freely off the ship, and I want to make you see that you have nothing to fear from me." "I will make sure you do not get into trouble from the white officers for leaving the ship,*" he added.

Akash felt that he had no choice but to agree and a part of him felt a surge of excitement at the thought of going offshore and into a tavern. He nodded to Khan in agreement, and they set off towards the dockside.

Khan led Akash offshore and through the busy dockside with its still bustling workers and through to a tavern on the far edge of the docks called the Rusty Anchor. He found himself bustled through the crowded bar room into a quiet alcove towards the back of the Tavern. Khan smiling warmly at Akash, ushered a barmaid over and looking at her lecherously, ordered a couple of tankards of ale and some brandy for himself and Akash.

"*Let's converse in English,*" Khan said. "*We don't want to seem discourteous to the others in the bar,*" he said. Akash, although having a grasp of English that was better than the average lascar, was not completely confident, but nodded in agreement.

"*Are you hungry Akash?*" Khan asked.

Akash, his stomach now grumbling in protest at the lack of food, nodded.

Khan replied, "*worry not lad, I will order a selection of food that you will not forget,*" he said chuckling.

Akash's earlier wariness of Khan started to subside as he was urged to down a tankard of ale with a brandy chaser. Akash had drunk before, but not in the volume he was drinking, and he felt a warm glow rise in his body from the ale and brandy. He listened to the stories regaled by Khan, but with each sip of ale and brandy, his head started to swim.

Shortly afterwards, a tray of food arrived with fresh oysters, a hearty stew with mutton and dumplings, bread, butter and cheese. Akash had never seen a feast such as this and his mouth watered at the very sight and smells of the food before him.

Khan, watching him closely, clapped him on his shoulders and said, "*Eat, my friend, this is the start of your new life of wealth,*" he added.

The words jolted Akash from the heady mix of alcohol and rich food. He looked at Khan and said in a quiet voice, "*I still feel guilty about my role and what happened to Sir Reginald, and that the suspicion that has fallen upon Arun,*" he said meekly.

Khan restraining his anger and urge to grab hold of Akash, sighed, took a deep breath and spoke. "*Do not torture yourself my friend, the death of Sir Reginald was an accident and Arun is no longer under suspicion. You have not hurt anyone and your role in all of this will bring you wealth with which you can help your family and better yourself,"* he said in an attempt to sound reassuring.

Akash considered Khan's words and decided to change the subject. *"This food is not like ours, but good Kabir, thank you."*

"No need to thank me, Akash," Khan replied. *"It is your good deeds that has brought you here and it's only the beginning,"* he ended, looking at Akash with the most reassuring and humble look he could muster.

The next hour flew by in a heady mix of conversation and an endless supply of ale and brandy. Akash suddenly started to feel nauseous and very lightheaded and did not register that they were joined at the table by a couple of rough looking men, both white and not the least bit friendly.

Khan broke the silence by greeting the two men. It was clear that he knew them. He offered a drink to both men and proceeded to introduce Akash as a good friend of his from the ship.

"Mr Topley and Mr Styles, meet up friend Akash" Khan said with an exaggerated show of good nature.

The two men acknowledged Akash with a perfunctory nod and turned to speak to Khan. Akash, with his head swimming and the noise of the Tavern, could not follow the conversation between Khan and his two compatriots, but sensed it was conspiratorial.

Something inside Akash told him that he should return to the Bengal and started to rise when Khan laid a hand on him to usher him to remain. *"What is the matter, Akash? Are you not enjoying the hospitality I have shown you?"* he said pointedly.

Despite the fog that was enveloping his mind, he was conscious that he did not want to insult Khan. *"No, Kabir, I thought I would leave you and these two gentlemen to speak privily,"* Akash said to be seen as being considerate.

"Nonsense!" shouted Khan in a jovial voice. *"Mr Topley and Mr Styles are in fact about to take their leave of us, they just dropped in to say hello to me,"* said Khan.

With that, the two gentlemen rose and left the table without uttering a word.

Khan smiled at Akash and said, *"One last round of drinks before we head back then."*

Akash, already feeling intoxicated did not know whether he could manage another drink, but his reluctance to annoy Khan meant that he nodded and stayed.

After consuming the last jug of ale and the last sip of brandy, Akash felt like his head had been hit with a hammer. He felt a mix of nausea, dizziness and inability to control his movements, which were bewildering and disconcerting.

In comparison, Khan seemed to have been unaffected by the copious amounts of alcohol that had been consumed. Khan looked intently at Akash and the smile that washed over him was that of pure evil.

Akash stood up and promptly fell as his legs failed to answer the demands made upon them. Khan caught Akash and picked him up and in front of a watching crowd, said with laughter, *"Come brother, time to head back to our ship."* With that, he hauled Akash through the tavern and out into the bitterly cold street which was covered in a blanket of thick fog.

Time seemed to evaporate and held no meaning for Akash as he was hauled by Khan through a myriad of streets. Akash had no sense of direction or where he was but was trying to contain the wave of nausea rising inside him. A short while later he realised that they were in a narrow alley and the noises he had heard from the hustle of men, women and children had died. An unearthly quiet had descended around them. Akash despite his inebriation, felt a surge of fear race through him. He tried to look at Khan and his surroundings through the fog in his eyes to ascertain where he was, but his sight was just a blur of shapes and shadows.

Suddenly, he felt many hands haul him into a deserted corner of an alley and pin him against the wall. A vicious punch to his stomach made him collapse in pain, but he was held up again as another blow rained on his head and then another to his stomach. Akash was awash with terror and pain as he fought to gather his thoughts. He felt blood seep into his mouth and realised that he had lost a tooth.

He tried to work his tongue to produce words and managed to cry out *"Stop, why?"*

A voice then boomed out as though Satan himself had risen from Hell. *"You are nothing more than a maggot, boy. Do you think I brought you out to spend money on you because we were friends,"* The voice rasped, dripping with indignation and malice.

Akash was struggling to take in what he heard through the fog of alcohol, fear and beating. He was fairly sure it was Khan, but before he could respond a torrent of blows rained down on him. Akash felt the burning pain course through his body, he felt bones crack, one eye close and more teeth loosen from his mouth, with the iron taste of blood trickling down his throat. Akash felt himself slipping into a darkness and blessed relief from the pain, but Khan and his confederates were not finished.

As Akash felt his mind slipping into darkness, he saw visions of his mother, siblings and the warmth of the sun from his homeland. It provided a degree of comfort as he knew deep down that his fate was sealed. Akash allowed himself to be taken by the coma-like darkness that was enveloping him. As he started to slide down into a heap on the floor, blood seeping from various parts of his body, his slide into oblivion and thus salvation from conscious pain was shattered by pails of cold icy water being thrown over him.

The bitter freezing water shook Akash from his slipping into darkness. He woke up in dazed confusion, eyes darting around seeking comprehension as to what was happening.

A soft, but terrifying voice whispered into his ears, thick with a pungent smell of alcohol, oysters and tobacco. *"I'm not ready to let you go you bastard,"* said the voice. *"You have only yourself to blame for this. You just could not be trusted to keep your mouth shut,"* the voice growled. The voice, which could only be that of Khan, continued. *"You have one last service to do me,"* he hissed menacingly.

Akash was beyond the ability to answer or comprehend the meaning behind the statement. He felt himself being dragged and then raised up on a post. He felt hands tie his feet and hands to the pole, the wrenching movement of the ropes causing searing pain in his hands, legs and shoulders. More water was thrown on his face to keep Akash from fainting.

The imposing face of Khan looked into Akash, as he grabbed his face roughly and spoke, *"this will serve as a warning to others, so I thank you for that,"* he said.

Akash, filled with terror, tried to speak, but could only mumble at Khan, imploring him to show mercy. Akash felt his shirt being ripped open to show his chest. He prayed to God, begging him to rescue him from this horror. From the corner of his one open eye, Akash saw the flash of a blade and then a searing pain as it cut through his chest and down to his stomach. Finally, and mercifully, Akash slipped into darkness as the laughter and brutal voices around him faded.

CHAPTER 10: SORROW

Blackthorn was awoken shortly after dawn by a barrage of hammering on his front door and opened it to find a breathless Constable scarcely able to compose his words.

"What is it, man? Blackthorn bellowed irritably.

The Constable composed himself and blurted out, *"There's been a murder guv, 'horrible."*

"Get a hold of yourself, Constable" Blackthorn commanded as he ushered the Constable into his house. *"I will go and ready myself and when I return, I want you to tell me everything you know,"* he said, turning in haste tohis bedroom.

The Constable was left standing in the narrow hallway of the Inspector's house, rubbing his face whilst composing his thoughts. Soon after, the Inspector returned and said, *"Lead the way, Constable. Take me to scene of the crime and on the way, tell me all you know."*

They walked quickly to the site of the murder, the Constable regaling the Inspector on all that he knew, which was not much other than where the body was found. As they approached the street where the body was found, the Inspector was confronted by a crowd of people who had gathered around the corpse. He pushed his way through the crowd, annoyed at the desecration of the crime scene.

The scene that confronted Blackthorn was straight out of a Penny Dreadful horror story(?). He gasped as he saw the mutilated body of a lascar. His face and body, swollen, was a mass of bruised and torn tissue, but the horrifying spectacle was that of the man's chest and stomach, which was slit open like a carcass in an abattoir to reveal his entrails and organs.

In all the time as inspector, Blackthorn had not witnessed such brutality, even amongst the worst scum he had arrested. The body was purposefully placed where it would been seen by the, and news of the horror would be carried back to the ships in the harbour and the taverns in every by lane and alleyway within several miles through a grapevine of increasingly exaggerated stories.

"Get rid of the gawkers, Constables," Blackthorn shouted as rage and revulsion rose in his body. *"I want only police here. Get to it!"* he bellowed at the Constables, who scrabbled to do his bidding.

Blackthorn's mind was racing. The fact that the body was obviously that of a lascar seemed to point at the events on the HMS Bengal, but the man could have come from any one of the ships moored at the Harbour. He needed the assistance of Arun, who may be able to help him identify the victim and point him in the right direction regarding the investigation.

Blackthorn turned to the Constable nearest to him and ushered him over. *"I want you to fetch a man called Arun Verma,"* he said in an urgent voice to the Constable.

The Constable stared at Blackthorn, trying to work out why the Inspector needed the assistance of a foreigner.

"Don't just stand there with your mouth open, Constable" Blackthorn hissed in annoyance. *"Here is the address where you will find Mr Verma., Bring him back as quickly as you can and without relaying any of the details of what has occurred here., Just tell him that Inspector Blackthorn needs his assistance."*

The Constable still with a confused expression on his face, said, *"Yes, Sir,"* and headed off through the outlying crowd to fetch Arun.

Blackthorn turned to the gruesome sight of the man strapped to the pole and ordered one of the other Constables to cut his binds and lay him on the ground. Blackthorn ignoring the bile rising in his stomach knelt to examine the body. He summoned up all his experience to remain calm and to look at the body dispassionately to discover any clues as to the identity of the man or reason for his violent death.

The man looked young and had no valuables on him, suggesting a robbery, but given the state of his clothes, Blackthorn dismissed the idea as this man was clearly not wealthy. The manner of his death suggested that the attack was premeditated and personal.

Blackthorn spent the next 15 minutes examining every part of the man's body and the surrounding area. There were multiple foot marks suggesting that this attack was not carried out by just one man. Blackthorn also noticed a trail of blood which ran from the pole and headed outwards to where the crowd stood, suggesting that the body was dragged to this point from elsewhere. Blackthorn cursed under his breath at the presence of the crowd who had no doubted trampled on any outlying evidence. Blackthorn continued his examination, and his concentration was only broken by the returning Constable.

"*I have fetched Mr Verma,*" he said with an air of accomplishment.

Blackthorn looked up, dismissed the Constable and gave a weary look to Arun. Arun sensed that something terrible had occurred here as he approached Blackthorn.

"*Arun, this is not a happy meeting,*" Blackthorn began, "*There has been a terrible murder and I think it is a* Lascar," he ended, looking thoughtfully at Arun.

Arun's attention was immediately drawn to the body that lay on the ground beside Blackthorn. He had not registered it before and moved closer to look at the bloodied and crumpled body that lay there. Arun winced as he saw the tortured body and squinted hard to recognise the face. His mind was a mix of fear, sorrow and incomprehension at what he saw before him. Blackthorn remained silent, allowing Arun to take in the scene before him.

"Do you recognise him?" Blackthorn asked gently.

Arun shook his head and then something told him to look more closely. Summoning up the courage to examine the wretched corpse, he knelt and stared at the face of the man that lay there. Slowly, recognition registered in Arun's mind. He felt his stomach lurch, and, without warning, he vomited next to the body of the dead man. Blackthorn startled by this, moved closer and patted Arun on the shoulder.

After a few minutes, Arun turned, tears streaming down his face and with a muted voice said, *"I think this is my friend Akash."* The very act of saying these words filled Arun with a wave of remorse and guilt. He reached over and, touching Akash's face, muttered a silent prayer and then said, *"This is all my fault."*

Blackthorn waved away the other Constables that approached to see what was happening. He knelt beside Arun and said, *"I am so sorry Arun. This is not your fault, but that of sadistic killers."*

"Killers?" Arun asked, his mind now filling with anger at what Akash had endured. *"You think Akash was killed by more than one person?"* he asked.

"The evidence points to that," Blackthorn replied. *"Now we know that the murdered man was Akash, everything points back to those on board the HMS Bengal,"* Blackthorn added.

Arun was startled out of his grief by what Blackthorn had said.

"I want to help find the killers," Arun stated. *"Akash may not have died if I hadn't been seen speaking with him yesterday, but the least I owe him is to find out who killed him and why,"* he concluded with a tone of grim determination.

Blackthorn looked at Arun closely and said, *"I understand, but we need to keep a clear head if we are to successfully find our killers and gather the evidence to see them hang,"* Arun turned to Blackthorn and, with a look that spoke of a deep resolve to see justice done for his friend, said, *"I understand"*.

CHAPTER 11: THE CHASE

Blackthorn decisively commanded his Constables to transport Akash's body to the morgue, insisting on an immediate autopsy by the Police Surgeon. He also instructed the meticulous collection of testimonies from the early witnesses of the horrendous scene. Fuelled by a fierce blend of rage and determination, Blackthorn, accompanied by Arun, embarked on an exhaustive inquiry through the neighbourhood's crumbling edifices, residences, and taverns.

Their journey through various locales unveiled the swift and rampant spread of the nightmarish tale of Akash's demise. The gory details, festering in the cauldron of local gossip, threatened to compromise the integrity of their investigation. Blackthorn, grudgingly aware of the city's appetite for tales marinated in horror, desired a fleeting grace period before the incident's cruel narration invaded London's streets and taverns. Hours were spent in relentless pursuit of substantial leads, engaging with locals and informants, only to end up with nothing more than gossip and conjecture which took them no further in their investigation.

Undeterred, their path, woven with threads of hope and frustration, eventually led them to the foreboding threshold of the Rusty Nail Tavern. Known to Blackthorn as a breeding ground of criminality, the tavern loomed as a potential crucible of concealed truths and clandestine tales. They entered an already bustling Tavern full of people having their midday repast of ale and an assortment of rancid looking dishes intermingled with appetising freshly cooked food, which catered for people of varying wealth.

Blackthorn realising that he had not breakfasted ushered Arun to a table and ordered some ale and food. Despite the events of the morning, they both ate ravenously when the food arrived and sated, they slumped on their chairs, consumed by their own thoughts.

Blackthorn broke the silence and asked Arun, *"Did Akash often frequent the taverns?"*

Arun immediately shook his head and said that he had never know Akash to leave the ship. *"Every penny he had, he saved for his family,"* Arun said mournfully.

Blackthorn anticipated this answer and surmised, *"So he was led off the ship by someone he knew or trusted, lured by the thought of food and ale, or maybe forcibly removed from the ship?"* Blackthorn pondered.

At that moment, a serving bar girl approached them and asked whether they wanted anything else.
Arun, suddenly inspired, asked the girl to take a seat for a moment to speak with them. The girl narrowed her eyes trying to gauge what this strange pair of a respectable-looking white man and a dark stranger wanted from her. Blackthorn reached for his warrant card, but Arun stayed him with a look and slight shake of his head.

Blackthorn smiled and said, *"My friend here just wants a quick chat, nothing more,"* and slid a shilling towards her. The girl's eyes widened in greed at the sight of the coin She swiftly swept it into her hand and sat down.

Arun, putting on his most amiable smile and demeanour, turned to the girl and said, *"I am seeking my friend who was out in the taverns last night. He is of my kind and would easily stand out in the crowd. Did you see anyone like that last night?"* he tailed off with a warm smile.

The girl's eyes brightened, and she responded, *"Yes, I did see someone like you. He was with another darkie, sorry….,"* the girl paused, searching for the correct term when Arun replied, *"Do carry on."*

"*Well, as I said, there were two gentlemen - one big, mean-looking with a turban and bushy beard, and another who looked more like you,*" the girl explained looking at Arun.

"*Where were the sitting?*" Arun continued, a sense of excitement building inside him at the description of the two men.

"*Why, here where you are sitting, sirs,*" the girl replied.

"*Did they seem like friends?*" Blackthorn interjected.

"*I don't know if they were friends, Sir, but the large man bought expensive oysters, meats with several tankards of ale and a bottle of Brandy, so I guess they must have been friendly,*" she mused.

"*How long did they stay here? Did anyone else join them?*" Arun asked trying to contain his eagerness.

The girl narrowing her eyes again looked between Blackthorn and Arun and said, "*Why do you want to know all of this?*" in a tone tinged with distrust and fear.

Blackthorn produced his Warrant Card and showed it to the girl. She visibly backed away and looked around the Tavern in sudden fear. She caught sight of the Landlord staring at her. "*I best get on with my duties, Inspector or I am likely to get a beating,*" she said in a voice beseeching them to let her go.

Blackthorn and Arun in unison said, "*Just one last question - were the two gentlemen you saw last night joined by anyone else?*"

At this moment a booming voice shouted across the Tavern, "*You get your arse over here girl and help out or by God, I will give you a hiding you won't forget!*" The girl flinched and they all turned to see the Landlord glaring at them.

Arun gently placed his hands on the girl's arm as she stood up to leave and whispered, "*Well, was there anyone else who joined the two lascars?*" he asked, imploring the girl to answer.

The girl, her face pink with fear, nodded and said in a barely audible whisper, "*Yes, two white dock hands, but they were only here for half an hour before they left.*"

"*Thank you,*" Arun said in a genuinely appreciative tone.

The girl collected their plates and tankards and hurried back to the Bar.

"*Well done!*" Blackthorn said after the girl had left, "*that was clever thinking Arun.*"

Arun smiled and said, "*Well we now know who Akash was with... Khan,*" he said with a note of anger.

Blackthorn nodded, "*We can guess what happened. Akash was lured to this Tavern by Khan, plied with copious amounts of alcohol and food until he was heavily drunk and then taken to some back alley where Khan was met by his two confederates, and they proceed to beat and murder Akash.*"

Arun flinched at Blackthorn's words and felt a wave of pity and grief rush through his body.

Blackthorn, oblivious to Arun's discomfort, went on. "*The question is why was Akash killed by Khan?*" he muttered, to himself.

Arun remembering his conversation on the ship, said, "*I am convinced that Akash was holding something back from me when we spoke. He and Khan were connected in some way and Akash was wracked with guilt about it*" Arun replied.

"*Yes, that makes sense, but what was it?*" Blackthorn considered.

"*It will be about money,*" Arun started, "*I pray to God it's not do with the murder of Sir Reginald,*" Arun tailed off looking thoughtful.

"*Come, we must find Khan and speak with him. The key to unlocking the murders of Sir Reginald and Akash lies with him,*" Blackthorn said, his voice filled with determination and grit.

With that, Blackthorn and Arun rose and left the tavern. They pushed their way through the mass of people, carts and hawkers, avoiding slipping on dung-ridden pathways to reach the dock where HMS Bengal was moored. They ran up the plank and onto the top deck of the ship.

They were met by a couple of surly officers who demanded to know what they wanted, and one asked a deck hand to call for Chief Middleton. Blackthorn was in no mood to be obstructed by anyone on this.

He said in a loud voice that brooked no dissention, *"I am looking for Mr Khan, kindly summon him or show me where I can find him. This is official Scotland Yard business,"* he emphasised.

The two junior officers looked at one another, unsure as to what to do or say. At that moment, Middleton arrived on the top deck. *"Inspector Blackthorn, it appears you cannot stay off this ship. Are you thinking of joining Mr Verma as a deck hand?"* he said in a mocking tone.

Blackthorn fixed Middleton with steely eyes and said, *"I am assuming you are aware that one of your crew, Mr Akash was found dead in the early hours of this morning?"*

Middleton, feigning surprise, said, *"I have been made aware of the disappearance of a* lascar *and instigated a search, but the news of his death was unknown to me until now Inspector."*

Blackthorn did not believe a word that Middleton said and pushed on. *"I would like to see Mr Khan immediately,"* he said to Middleton.

Middleton sensing that the Inspector was in no mood to be hindered, turned to one of the officers and said, *"Fetch Mr Khan.*

Arun, observing the exchange between Blackthorn and Middleton sensed that Middleton's demeanour was that of a man who was desperately trying to hide his anxiety and he wondered why. Arun continued to stare at Middleton when the officer commanded to fetch Khan came back looking flustered. Standing in front of Middleton, he said nervously, *"Sir, we cannot find Khan and he was seen by a couple of the deck hands, disembarking the ship earlier this morning."*

Both Arun and Blackthorn noticed that Middleton's initial reaction was that of a man unsurprised by the news, but then he put on a façade of a man gripped by anger. Shouting at the officer, he said, *"What do you mean he has disembarked the ship, how can you let this happen, officer?"* he bellowed.

The officer shrank into himself at Middleton's words. Middleton turned around to Blackthorn and with an expression of regret said, *"I am sorry, Inspector, it seems that Khan has absconded and will be dealt with severely."*

Blackthorn, clearly unimpressed, stared at Middleton, turned on his heels and together with Arun stormed off the ship.

As Blackthorn and Arun left the ship, they both shared their opinions on what just happened. Once they were onshore, Blackthorn turned to Arun and with a voice that barely contained his anger, *"Khan has clearly been told about the body of Akash being discovered and our investigation. I feared his snouts would relay the news to him. He will not be returning to the ship but will be trying to find a place to hide nearby. We must hunt him down, Arun,"* Blackthorn rasped, beating his fist, in frustration, on a sack of grain that was next to him.

Arun clapped his hands on Blackthorn's shoulder and said with a reassurance he did not feel, *"we will find him and bring him to justice, Inspector."*

Arun and Blackthorn waded through the backstreets of the docks and nearby shadowy quarters of workers, hawkers, thieves, whores and opium dens in search of a scent of where Khan was hiding. Blackthorn was like a man driven by rage and righteous zeal to avenge the murders of Sir Reginald and Akash. He turned to every snout he had and tolerated no dissembling or resistance from them. Using the threat of violence and retribution of the law, he gleaned every ounce of information that was known to his snouts in the streets.

Arun too felt the thrill of the chase within him and used his native language to speak with other lascars and merchants from the East to find out if they knew where Khan was. Khan was well known to amongst other lascars and traders from India, and they were scared and keen to help in equal measure.

They had to distil multiple sightings of Khan and had no choice but to pursue all leads, regardless of their scepticism of the value of the information they had gleaned. By now, Blackthorn and Arun knew, word of their search for Khan would have spread through the alleyways and taverns. As dusk fell upon them, the dimming light cast eerie shadows as Blackthorn and Arun continued their search, ignoring their aching bodies and empty stomachs in their desperation to land their prey. As they turned into a foreboding looking alleyway which led to a tavern and an opium den, they found themselves ensnared in a trap.

Like vipers in the dark, the two towering and menacing figures of Topley and Styles stepped in front of them, each holding a club and knife with murderous looks on their faces. Behind the vicious duo stood the unmistakable form of Khan, a malicious grin spreading across his face. Blackthorn and Arun gripped by fear stood rooted to the spot, staring at the two men and Khan behind them. Blackthorn's mind worked frantically trying to summon up his training and experience to construct a plan of defence. Arun suddenly felt very calm.

The events of the past few days had taken its toll on his mind and body, and the face of his brutalised friend suddenly appeared to him. Arun decided then that he would not cower and plead for mercy. If this were his time to die, he would do so fighting, in the memory of his friend and to honour his father. Whilst he felt a wave of sadness at the thought of leaving his family, he resigned himself to whatever fate had planned for him.

Then a voice, cold and menacing, rang out from the cloud of fog that began to descend upon them. *"You really are a like a dog with bone, Inspector, you just won't go away,"* Blackthorn and Arun spun around in unison to see the figure of Middleton, gun in one hand pointing at them.

Blackthorn and Arun found themselves speechless. Middleton sensing this, laughed. *"It's good to see your face so confused and shocked, Inspector"* he hissed. *"The famous Inspector from Scotland Yard, with his dumb coolie, stuck for words,"* he crowed.

Blackthorn composing himself, straightened his back and stared back at Middleton, *"Surprised? No,"* Blackthorn began. *"It's the age-old story of a man tired of waiting for his superior to retire and wanting to hasten his demise so he can earn the stripes of a Captain,"* Blackthorn stated as though this whole affair was not a mystery of any kind.

Middleton momentarily paused, wondering how much Blackthorn knew, then smirked and replied, *"If you think this whole affair has been about me gaining promotion to Captain, then you are more stupid than I thought,"* he rasped.

Blackthorn ignoring Middleton's response went on. *"I assume the last part of your plan is to kill Arun and I and make it look like we were set upon by some ruffians?"* Blackthorn enquired.

"Something like that," Middleton responded calmly. *"I can see you are desperate to know the full story,"* Middleton gloated. *"Well since you both haven't much longer to live, there is no harm in sharing the tale,"* Middleton said with a look of perverse pleasure.

Khan roared at this point, *"No! let's just kill them and be on our way Saib,"* he urged Middleton.

Middleton with a look of irritation snapped at Khan, *"Just shut your face and do as you are told,"* he admonished Khan.

Topley and Styles moved forward toward Middleton as though they were offended by Middleton's response to Khan.

"Keep you dogs on their leash, Khan, or you won't see a penny from this enterprise," Middleton hissed.

Khan calmed his two compatriots and stood staring at Middleton. Middleton undeterred from Khan's interruption turned to Blackthorn and Arun and with a smile said, *"this is all about money, Blackthorn, more than you would see in 10 lifetimes,"* he emphasised.

Blackthorn did not respond, allowing Middleton to gloat whilst he considered the options for getting through this alive. *"I was tired of being a lapdog to Sir Reginald and together with a friend in a shipping insurance company came up with the idea of scuttling the HMS Bengal and diverting the insurance money due to the East India Company into our own pockets before anyone had realised."*

Middleton was frothing at the mouth from the excitement of recanting the plan. He went on, *"I recruited Khan as I knew he had deep gambling debts and needed to pay off people who could do him damage if he did not make good on his debts. We never planned to kill Reginald in the way he was, but wanted to steal the contents of the safe which held a tidy sum. The idiot Khan chose the lascar, Akash to steal the contents of the safe for which he would get a small share of the loot."*

Arun's mouth opened at this revelation from Middleton, which pleased Middleton.

"You are all thieves Verma, no need to show surprise," Middleton sneered.

Blackthorn interjected and said, *"So what happened then, Middleton?"*

With a smile, Middleton continued. *"I stole some papers from Sir Reginald's cabin prior to the theft from the safe to create an impression that there was a plot to steal important papers. That old fool, Sir Reginald, bought this story and sought to protect all the papers he held."*

With a guttural laughter, Middleton went on, *"On the night that Akash was to enter Sir Reginald's cabin and steal the contents of the safe, I had stolen the keys to the safe and left it open for Akash. I told Akash what time to enter Sir Reginald's cabin, but the coolie lost track of time, and Sir Reginald discovered him in the cabin. I heard the commotion that ensued and, afraid that it would alert the attention of the night guards, I entered Sir Reginald's cabin to find a whimpering Akash, kneeling on the floor, hands clasped in subjugation."*

Middelton, eyes bulging and clearly revelling in telling his tale went on, *"I knew it was only a matter of time before Akash would spill his guts out to Sir Reginald so I grabbed the nearest heavy object I could find and struck Sir Reginald from behind. He fell immediately, but he was not dead, just concussed. I told Akash to return to his bunk and not to speak to anyone if he valued his life and wanted a share of the money. Once he left, a plan formed in my mind, I headed to find a knife from the kitchen that Arun used, returned and stabbed Sir Reginald until he was dead."* Middleton was breathless from telling his story and took and deep breath to recover.

"So, you planned to lay the blame on me and see me hanged," asked Arun.

Middleton laughed and said, *"Did you think you were special coolie? Sir Reginald thought you a useful person to have onboard. To me, you were nothing but a convenient scapegoat,"* he said coldly.

Anger grew inside Arun, and he clenched his fists tightly.

Middleton noticing this, sighed and said, *"I am bored with this., Khan, you and your men do what you need to do. I will enjoy this,"* he said menacingly.

Blackthorn instinctively made a lunge at Middleton hoping to catch him unawares, but Middleton was too quick and raised his gun, pointing it at Blackthorn's face. *"Now, Inspector, I do not want to shoot you, but I will. Just be a man and take your beating,"* he said with a laugh. Middleton looked at Khan, signalling to him to continue.

Then with lightning speed that belied their huge frames, Topley and Styles struck, their intent lethal and determination chilling. These were men moulded in Khan's merciless image, with orders to obliterate any hindrance. They went for Blackthorn first and for all his storied prowess, he found himself cornered. He braced himself for the undoubted blows that would follow.

Khan in the meantime moved towards Arun with a malevolent grin, his dagger shining in the dim lights around them.

There followed what seemed like a coordinated dance as Khan, Topley and Styles edged closer to their prey, moving in a circle to close on their victims. Blackthorn was no stranger to street fights and was more than handy with his fists. He eyed the smaller of Khan's agents and with a swift movement which took Styles by surprise, he summersaulted on the ground avoiding the blows that were targeted on him and, pulling out a penknife from his pocket, he lunged it deeply into the thigh of Styles.

He roared with pain and surprise. His leg crumpled and he dropped his club and knife. Topley suddenly feeling less sure of himself, ran at Blackthorn, his eyes blazing with anger and a guttural roar emanating from within him. Time seemed to stand still, and Khan, Arun and Middleton felt themselves fixed to where they stood, watching the events unfold. Blackthorn grabbed the knife lying next to the bloodied man he had stabbed and rolled on to his feet. He dodged the first blow from Topley who was running towards him and delivered a thumping kick to his groin. Topley screamed with agony but kept coming for Blackthorn.

At the same time, Arun, sensing that Khan was distracted, moved to one side and summoning up all the anger and grief he felt, swung his hands and landed a heavy punch on the side of Khan's neck. Khan staggered back, surprised by the attack and looked at Arun with pure hatred. He gripped his dagger and lunged for Arun. Arun swaying, his wiry body moving with the speed of a cobra, bent and picked up a handful of wet mud and filth from the ground and hurled it at Khan. His aim was true, and it hit Khan in the eyes.

Middleton now in a state of panic at the unexpected turn of events pulled back the trigger to his gun and aimed it at Arun. Arun, sensing this kept moving and ducking to make himself a more difficult target. He felt a bullet fly past his head like a killer bee buzzing to bite its victim.

Khan had rubbed the dirt off his eyes and, while his vision was compromised, he focused on Arun and ran towards him. As a further shot rang through the air, Arun, fearing the searing pain of a bullet or Khan's dagger used all his fleeting speed to move away from Khan and avoided the first of his blows with the dagger. Khan roared with anger and frustration as Arun continued to duck and weave. From the corner of his eye, Arun saw Middleton lift his gun, tracking Arun's movement to find his true aim.

As Khan and Arun moved in a dance of death, Arun suddenly heard the shot from Middleton's gun, and he braced himself for its deathly impact. However, at that very moment, Khan consumed by the desire to kill Arun moved in front of him to apply the final slash of his dagger. The bullet smashed into the back of Khan and through his chest into the brickwork next to Arun. Khan stared at Arun in disbelief as blood gushed out of his chest. His arms dropped, the dagger clanging onto the ground and Khan slumped to his knees. With final look at Arun, he slumped forward and crashed onto the ground.

Arun gasped as Khan fell and he looked at Middleton. Middleton growled with rage and walked towards Arun, reloading his gun and pining Arun down with his fierce gaze. Arun braced himself for fate had decided that his end would be here, amongst the filth and degradation of this alleyway. Arun closed his eyes and let his mind wander to see the faces of his family, his beloved Priya and the dusty, warm land of his birth. He was prepared to meet his fate and clung on to these visions as he prepared for the violent end that awaited him.

As Arun waited for his fate, an unnerving silence seemed to descend upon him. For a moment Arun wondered whether he was dead already. Suddenly he felt the sound of a gunshot and a screeching wail of pain accompanying it. Arun felt around his body searching for the bullet wound, his eyes still closed tightly. He slowly opened his eyes when he could not find a mortal wound to see Blackthorn standing above him with smile. *"Are you alive lad?"* he said with a chuckle. Arun feeling confused and dazed muttered, *"Is that you Blackthorn?"*

"Yes Arun, it is me. Who were you expecting to see?" Blackthorn retorted whilst he bent down to pick up Arun.

Arun, still confused, noticed the blood on Blackthorn's shoulder and a wound on his arm. *"Are you okay?"* Arun asked.

Blackthorn slapped Arun on his back and said, *"Yes, I am fine, you?"*

"I am okay, I think," replied, Arun. *"What about Middleton?"* Arun went on, suddenly remembering the man with the gun.

"Whilst you were doing your impression of a Cobra and trying to stay alive, I snuck behind Middleton and before he could aim at you properly, I hit him on his head." Middleton replied.

"Is he dead?" Arun asked.

"No, he is alive and bound," said Blackthorn. *"He will wake up in a few hours, by which time he will be behind bars, and will no doubt have an appointment with the hangman to answer for his crimes,"* Blackthorn

said with a tone of satisfaction.

"What about Khan's agents?" Arun went on, eager to piece together all that had happened.

Blackthorn looked at him and with a smile said, *"You are like a detective, Arun, seeking all the answers to conclude a case. One of the agents is over there lying in a pool of his own blood and the other ran away when he realised that I would not be as easy to kill as he had thought,"* he said with a smile.

"Now, enough of the questions. Help me get these two criminals to Scotland Yard and after the Police Doctor has seen us, we deserve a bloody strong drink and some food," exclaimed Blackthorn.

CHAPTER 12: NEW BEGININGS

In the following days, the news of the case and the capture of Middleton spread like wildfire across the city and the country at large. Every newspaper and pamphlet had detailed and increasingly dramatised tales of the events that had unfolded over the course of a few days. The successful resolution of the case brought much kudos to Blackthorn and Scotland Yard, and even a reward from The East India Company who were more relieved that they did not lose a ship and less concerned with the lives that were lost. The role played by Arun Verma was less widely reported and acknowledged, appearing in some publications as a mere footnote to Blackthorn.

Blackthorn to his credit and Arun's appreciation did not belittle the help he received from Arun. At every opportunity, whether it be with his superiors at the Yard or to reporters, he made sure that Arun's role was given prominence, and he openly praised the help he had received.

"Arun was instrumental in solving the case," he would say, ensuring everyone knew of Arun's significance.

Arun for his part was circumspect, his thoughts moving to what the future lay in store for him. That is not to say that he did not enjoy the praise and free ale that was bought by some Londoners in recognition of what he had done but as the days rolled on, he became increasingly anxious about the future. The East India company still owned him through the binds of their contract with him, but every sinew of Arun's mind and body rebelled at the thought of returning to HMS Bengal, and to spending his life on the seas.

His master's at the East India Company had invited him to meet with them and he was apprehensive as to what they wanted. He longed to speak with Blackthorn, but he had not seen him for several days as the Inspector was occupied with various legal and police duties he had since the arrest of the suspects and conclusion of the case or, worse still, Blackthorn had moved on now that the case was concluded, Arun brooded.

Arun often turned to Emily since the news of the case broke and whilst she was in awe of what he had been involved in, which made Arun a little embarrassed, she was kind and attentive in listening to Arun's thoughts and providing advice. Apart from Blackthorn, Emily was the only other friend and confidant that Arun had in London. She knew the hardships of making a life in this unforgiving city and therefore understood the travails of Arun's mind.

"Emily, I fear they might force me back to the seas," he confessed.

"You've proven yourself, Arun. Something good will come," Emily assured, comforting him.

The following evening, Arun found himself nestled in the worn armchair of his temporary abode, the warm glow of the hearth casting dancing shadows around the room. The fire crackled with a comforting ferocity, yet its embrace could not reach the chill of his thoughts. There he was, ensconced in the cosy parlour, a world away from the familiarity of home, grappling with the chilling events in which he had inadvertently become embroiled.

Arun wondered whether news of these dramatic events would ever reach the ears of his family or his beloved Priya? The urge to share every detail with his mother, whose gentle wisdom had always been his guiding star, was a palpable ache in his chest. Equally, the thought of Priya, with her keen intellect and compassionate spirit, being in the dark about his circumstances pained him. For forty-eight hours, the impulse to pour his thoughts onto paper had been battling with a paralysing uncertainty of how to encapsulate the chaos into words. Each time he poised his quill above the blank page, the enormity of his experiences stifled the words before they could take flight. His involvement in events that would seem too fantastical for bedtime stories to his younger siblings back home had left him at a loss for how to begin his letter.

Compounding his restlessness was the apprehension about the rendezvous that awaited him in the morning, the meeting with The East India Company, wondering whether he would be taken directly from the meeting to the HMS Bengal and back to his binds of servitude.

He was jolted out of his deep thoughts by Emily. *"You have a visitor"* she said with a knowing smile.

Before Arun could answer, a booming voice behind Emily said, *"Did you think I had forgotten about you?"* with a chuckle.

Arun instantly recognised the voice of Blackthorn and looked up to see him approach him, proffering a hand to shake. Arun's face broke out in a warm smile as he warmly shook the hand of Blackthorn. *"It's good to see you again,"* Arun said, a relieved look on his face.

There was a brief silence as Emily returned with drinks, placing them gently on the table. With a soft smile, she excused herself, leaving the two men to their conversation.

"I've been swamped, my friend," Blackthorn said apologetically. *"The case has brought a whirlwind of responsibilities."*

"I understand, but it's really good to see you," Arun replied, feeling a sense of comfort in his friend's presence.

Blackthorn sensed that something was worrying Arun and asked, *"Are you okay? You seem concerned?"*

"In the morrow, I meet with The East India Company," Arun voiced, a touch of anxiety lacing his words. *"I fear they aim to chain me back to the seas, to a life away from the possibilities this land has started*

unveiling." Blackthorn's face grew serious, his eyes reflecting understanding. "*It is a crossroads, indeed. But remember, you are not alone. We shall navigate through whatever comes your way.*"

Arun smiled, but his face now sombre and pensive went on, "*The thought of returning to HMS Bengal haunts me,*" Arun admitted, looking into the fire, as if seeking answers within its fierce, erratic dance. "*I've tasted freedom here, Blackthorn, felt the stirrings of a different future,*" he said with passion.

Blackthorn looked at his new friend with compassion, his mind considering the options that Arun could have. "*You've earned choices, Arun, the whole of London and certainly Scotland Yard know of your services to the community,*" Blackthorn said firmly, offering a supportive nod. "*Your fate is not etched in stone, and we will contest anything. Would you like me to accompany you to your meeting with the East India Company?*" Blackthorn asked.

Arun was taken by surprise at this offer and for a moment, he was lost for words. "*I don't know what to say except that I would be honoured if you would accompany me,*" Arun said.

"*Good, that is settled. What time is your meeting?*" Blackthorn asked, his voice reflecting a steely determination.

"*The meeting is scheduled for 10 o'clock at their offices,*" Arun responded.

"*Very well, I'll arrive here at 9 o'clock, and together we'll confront whatever challenges await us,*" Blackthorn declared, offering a smile of encouragement. "*But for now, I must bid you farewell; I have other responsibilities that require my attention,*" he concluded.

With that he stood up, shook Arun's had and moved to leave. Arun stayed him and with a genuine look of gratitude he said, "*thank you Blackthorn, you are a good friend.*"

Blackthorn smiled and without a further word left. Arun, alone again, felt a renewed sense of hope for what lay ahead and thanked

God for bringing him good friends such as Blackthorn and Emily. The next day Blackthorn arrived on time as promised and together they set off for the grand offices of the East India Company.

They arrived shortly before 10am and were ushered into an anteroom. The Clerk was surprised to see Blackthorn, but the introduction of him as a Scotland Yard Inspector prevented him from making any objections. Scarcely had the hour passed when the Clerk summoned Arun and Blackthorn to the quarters of the Chief Marshall of the East India Company. A middle-aged man of sour disposition, marked by a conspicuously inflamed nose indicative of habitual libation, acknowledged them with but a curt nod. With a gesture, he bade them take their seats in sumptuous armchairs arrayed before his grand oak table, which bore an array of nautical instruments and charts.

With a look of stark disapproval, the Chief Marshall's eyes bore into Blackthorn. *"I was under the impression that this interview was to be conducted solely with Mr. Verma. Pray tell, what business have you here?"* he inquired with marked acuity.

Blackthorn, undeterred and internally affirming his initial impression of the man's haughtiness, made his stance known in a pronounced formal tone. *"I am Inspector Blackthorn, in service of Scotland Yard,"* he declared, maintaining unyielding eye contact. *"It is due to Mr. Verma's significant contributions to our inquiries, which led to the apprehension of scoundrels responsible for not only the vilest of murders but conspiring to send your vessel to Davy Jones' Locker and defraud the insurers of a handsome sum,"* Blackthorn articulated, his lips curving into a subtle smirk.

The Chief Marshall, visibly struggling to rein in his pique, posed the question anew, *"I must press you, Inspector, to what purpose do you have in your presence today?"*

At this point Arun interjected. *"Sir, Inspector Blackthorn accompanies me in advocating for my release from the binds of my engagement with the East India Company,"* he professed, his voice tinged with apprehension.

"*Such a course is unthinkable,*" retorted the Chief Marshall brusquely. "*You have scarcely served twelve months of the five years to which you are obliged.*" At this decree, Arun felt the heavy shroud of despondency descend upon him.

Blackthorn adopted a posture of firm resolve, inflating his chest as if steeling himself for a skirmish. "*Pray, allow me to speak,*" he addressed the Chief Marshall. "*Were it not for Mr. Verma's intervention, your esteemed company would presently be embroiled in ignominy and financial ruination far outweighing any potential gain from his servitude over the span of five years.*"

The Chief Marshall made to interject, but Blackthorn forestalled him with a raised hand.

"*I beg you to permit me to finish. Should the East India Company elect to disregard Mr. Verma's considerable merits, it stands to be deemed callous in the court of public sentiment. Moreover, it is conceivable that the sordid tales of malfeasance and malevolence rampant upon your vessels could very well become the subject of fervent scrutiny and reportage by the press, voracious for scandal,*" he concluded.

The Chief Marshall's countenance turned a deep shade of red with vexation. Abruptly rising from his seat and looming over the desk, he bore down upon Blackthorn with a fierce glare, bellowing, "*Is this an attempt at coercion, sir? I shall see to it that such insolence costs you your station!*"

Yet Blackthorn remained serene, a placid smile on his visage as he extended his palms in a gesture of peace. "*I assure you; I proffer no blackmail. It is merely a counsel that any negative light cast upon the East India Company could incite the journalistic hounds to delve into the mire for lurid tales. And as for my employ, it would indeed appear most peculiar for the Company to seek the ousting of a Detective who has just recently unravelled a substantial conspiracy and thereby averted a considerable defrauding of your institution.*"

The Chief Marshall slowly sat down, leaning back on his chair considering what Blackthorn had said and how to respond. The air seemed charged with tension as the minutes passed by before the Chief Marshall, leaned forward and said in a quiet voice.

"So, you would like me to release Arun from the contract he has with us?" the Chief Marshall said, more as a statement to himself rather than a question.

Arun held his breath as he waited for the Chief Marshall to speak again. With a sarcastic smile, the Chief Marshall said, *"yes I think Mr Verma's contract can be terminated, and we can present it as a reward for his services, as you say Inspector, good publicity instead of bad"* his voice had a vindictive tone to it.

Both Arun and Blackthorn were confused at the tone of the Chief Marshall's response.

Before either could speak, the Chief Marshall added with a vicious expression, *"well I'm sure you know gentleman that without the patronage of the East India Company, Mr Verma's right to stay in London will be short lived under the immigration rules and he would be forced to find a passage back to India"*.

Arun and Blackthorn both fell silent, not having considered the ramifications of being released by the East India Company. Blackthorn looked at Arun trying to gauge his response. After several minutes of silence during which the Chief Marshall had nonchalantly continued his daily work, Arun stood up and cleared his throat. Both the Chief Marshall and Blackthorn looked up at him.

Arun, his voice strong and steady, spoke. *"Chief Marshall, I thank you for taking your valuable time to meet with me and having considered everything that has been said, I would like to accept the offer of my contract being terminated without any penalty. I would be happy to complete any paperwork before we leave your offices"* he finished.

Both Blackthorn and the Chief Marshall stared at Arun and whilst Blackthorn had a smile on his face, the Chief Marshall seemed genuinely shocked at Arun's decision.

"*Very well Mr Verma, is that is your decision, I will have the necessary legal documents drawn up for you to sign. Please wait in the anteroom.*"

Upon the Chief Marshall's dismissal, Blackthorn and Arun were ushered from the room. As Arun pivoted to exit the Chief Marshall's quarters, his legs wavered, threatening to give way beneath him. It took every ounce of his resolve not to crumple to the floor. Blackthorn, perceptive to his struggle, quickly reached out to steady Arun, cleverly disguising the supportive gesture as a congratulatory pat on the shoulder.

Once secluded in the adjoining chamber, a silence enveloped Arun and Blackthorn, each man ensnared by his own ruminations. It was only after a considerable pause that Arun broke the silence with a whisper, "*Your support has been invaluable; without it, I would still be under the East India Company's yoke.*"

A warm, understanding expression crossed Blackthorn's face as he responded, "*helping you was the least I could do after everything we've been through, my friend.*"

"*I'm at a loss for what comes next,*" Arun confessed, worry lacing his tone.

Lost in contemplation, Blackthorn regarded Arun and offered a ray of hope. "*Hang on to hope. I have been toying with a plan that might just be the solution we need,*" he revealed, prompting a spark of optimism in Arun's eyes. "*Nothing is certain yet, but give me a couple of days, and I'll return with more to tell,*" Blackthorn added.

Arun, driven by curiosity, pressed, "*Can't you share even a hint?*"

With a firm shake of his head, Blackthorn maintained, "*It has to remain under wraps for now, until I'm sure it's feasible. You'll have to trust me on this.*" Although frustration gnawed at him, Arun understood the futility of pressing Blackthorn further.

Time stretched on endlessly until finally, the Clerk stepped into the room, a bundle of papers gripped in his grasp. "*Mr. Verma, we've prepared all the necessary documents for your perusal,*" he stated, his voice devoid of interest. His gaze fleetingly met Arun's, signalling for him to come and finalise the paperwork in his office, taking a copy for his records as if the task were just another mundane item on his checklist.

As the Clerk made to guide Arun to his workspace, he hesitated with a question, "*Is there someone here to act as a witness for you?*" His eyes flickered between Arun and Blackthorn, uncertain of the bond they shared.

Before Arun could reply, Blackthorn chimed in with a supportive smile, "*I'd be honoured to witness the signing.*"

Within a mere quarter of an hour, Arun found himself in the hallway, clutching his freedom in the form of release papers from the East India Company. His emotions were a whirlwind of relief and unease.

Blackthorn gave him a congratulatory slap on the back. "*congratulations, the path to your new beginning is now open,*" he declared, his smile unwavering.

Exiting the building, they were greeted by the sting of a chilly wind and a drizzle that promised to deepen into rain. Blackthorn, facing Arun, inquired, "*Will you manage your way back? I must return to Scotland Yard.*"

Arun nodded, noting Blackthorn's earnest expression. "*Yes, I'll be fine. Might we meet later?*" he asked.

"*I can't be certain,*" Blackthorn admitted. "*But stay at your lodgings. I aim to bring you some news upon my return.*" With those parting words, he flagged down a hansom cab and disappeared in the direction of Scotland Yard.

Arun, undeterred by the chilling rain, chose to walk. He needed the time to reflect on Blackthorn's mysterious hint of a plan.

Arun trudged back to his lodgings, weariness in every step. The meandering cobbled streets and the grime-slicked alleys had given him ample time to brood over his uncertain future in this unfamiliar place.

Upon his arrival, Emily, with her ever-present smile, bustled up to greet him. *"You're back! Tell me everything!"* she exclaimed, leading him towards his room.

As they walked, Arun recounted the events of the morning. *"So, the papers are signed. I am no longer bound to the Company,"* he said, his voice carrying a hint of a sombre undertone.

Emily's face lit up like the dawn. *"That is incredible, Arun! You are free now, free to carve out your own destiny here!"* Her enthusiasm was palpable, yet it barely masked the lingering uncertainties that haunted him.

"Thank you, Emily. But freedom comes with its own chains," Arun sighed, the weight of his next steps in this foreign land pressing upon him.

Noticing his mood, Emily quickly changed the subject. *"You must be famished! Would you like something to eat? Some ale to wash it down?"*

"Yes, that would be good," Arun nodded, grateful for the distraction.

"Sit here. I will bring you something hearty," Emily said, guiding him to a cosy table before disappearing into the kitchen. She returned shortly with a tankard frothing with ale, a plate piled with bread, and a generous portion of cheese. *"Here you are. Eat up! It will make you feel better,"* she encouraged, her smile unwavering.

Arun needed no second bidding, diving into the simple meal with a vigour he did not know he possessed. With each bite, the cacophony in his mind began to quiet, giving way to a comforting numbness. Finishing his meal, he drained his tankard, the ale casting a warm haze over his worries.

"Thank you, Emily. This... this was much needed," he mumbled, feeling the exhaustion of the day finally catching up to him. Suddenly felt very tired, Arun decided to head up to his room and hope that sleep would envelope him and take him away from his worries.

Arun was jolted awake by a series of loud knocks on his door. Groggy and disoriented, he squinted in the darkness of the room, wondering, *"What time could it be?"*

Another round of knocks echoed, accompanied by Blackthorn's voice cutting through the silence, *"get up, Arun."*

"Give me just a moment, I'll be right there," Arun called back, trying to piece together the reason for such a disturbance. Stumbling down the stairs, Arun spotted Blackthorn at a table, a pair of ale-filled tankards before him.

"Very soon you won't have the luxury of sleeping whenever the mood takes you," Blackthorn teased, a playful glint in his eye.

Arun, puzzled, took a seat across from him. Blackthorn slid a tankard across the table and raised his own, *"We missed out on celebrating earlier, so here's to you, Arun."* As Arun lifted his drink, his curiosity about Blackthorn's news—and his cryptic remark about sleep—grew urgent.

Catching on to Arun's eagerness, Blackthorn began, *"Guess where I've been?"* Arun, growing a tad irritable with the suspense, simply shook his head. *"I've been in talks with the Chief Constable at Scotland Yard, and your name came up,"* Blackthorn disclosed.

Arun head jerked up, eyes wide, trying to gauge Blackthorn's expression, his heart pounding. *"Am I in some sort of trouble?"* he inquired, apprehensive.

Blackthorn chuckled before posing a question with a more solemn tone, *"How would you feel about becoming a Special Constable?"*

Arun was momentarily speechless, his face a canvas of astonishment and confusion. *"A Special Constable?"* he echoed.

With a nod, Blackthorn elaborated, *"It's an informal role for now. The Yard is not quite ready for someone of your unique background,"* he said, smiling warmly. *"You'd assist me with cases involving minority communities and function as a liaison with the* lascars."

"And will there be pay? A uniform?" Arun asked, the information slowly sinking in.

"Yes, you'll be paid less than a regular constable, I'm afraid, but it's still a decent wage, better than a ships, and it'll keep you in London," Blackthorn assured him.

Arun paused for a moment to align his thoughts. Visions of his mother, his siblings, and Priya drifted through his mind as he pondered his next steps. The offer from Blackthorn was undeniably a golden ticket, one that promised to reshape his future irrevocably. The dilemma of potentially leaving his family without the certainty of reunion weighed heavily on him. Amidst his internal struggle and uncertainty, Arun's thoughts drifted to the vow he had made to his late father — to safeguard his family and to provide them with every chance to improve their circumstances. The opportunity from Blackthorn held the potential to fulfil this promise, offering financial stability for his loved ones. And, if fate allowed, it might pave the way to reunite them all in London one day.

Arun, his mind resolved, stood up, straightened his back and offered his hand to Blackthorn. *"I would be delighted to become your*

Special Constable Inspector. I do not know how to thank you" he said with a warm smile. Blackthorn shook Arun's hand and said, *"good man, you start first thing tomorrow."*

EPILOGUE

Three months later, on the damp morning of February 14, 1857, a steady mist clung to London like a persistent malaise, yet the unyielding fog could not dampen the city's pulse. Since the first pale light of dawn, hordes had been converging on the capital — some trudging through muddied streets, others disembarking from the hissing steam of the rail, each person carried by a current of morbid fascination.

Such gatherings were typically reserved for the pomp of Queen Victoria's processions or the arrival of illustrious dignitaries, but today, the throng was magnetised by a far grimmer spectacle: the execution of the notorious Chief Middleton and his nefarious accomplices, Topley and Styles, all doomed to the gallows for their part in the murders. While the masses clustered in anticipation of the grim event, reporters from every corner of the city clamoured for the juiciest angle, desperate to pen a final story of this saga that would titillate their readers.

Two months prior, the press was ablaze with lurid and ghastly tales surrounding the notorious affair promoting sensational headlines in newspapers and pamphlets.

"Gentleman's Grisly Fate: Society in Shock as Prominent Figure Dangles from the Gallows!"

"Ghastly Discovery: Sidekick to Notorious Middleton Found Dead – Murder Most Foul?"

"End of the Line for Parkinson: Sudden Death – Justice's Cold Embrace or Guilt's Final Act?"

Through relentless interrogation of Middleton, Blackthorn unearthed Parkinson's involvement in the heinous scheme and subsequent murder. While concrete evidence tying Parkinson directly to the slayings remained elusive, his machinations to swindle the East India Company given the potential ruin of HMS Bengal were damning enough to possibly send him to the gallows. The tidings of Middleton's apprehension and the fall of his accomplices prompted Parkinson to take flight, yet it appeared that retribution, in the end, had ensnared him. Whether by the weight of his own conscience or another's deed, the truth would elude Blackthorn. Yet, to him, this was another riddle resolved in the grand enigma.

Neither Blackthorn nor Arun bore witness the public execution of Middleton, Topley and Styles, choosing instead to avoid the spotlight and the grim sights and sounds of the hanging.

At Scotland Yard, Blackthorn's office was a bastion of calm and quiet industry. Here, sat in the leather-bound world of paperwork and muted conversations, were Blackthorn and Arun, focused intently on the documents before them. Special Constable Arun, whose duty it was to sift through the myriad reports from informers, found solace in the challenge of piecing together the clandestine puzzles presented by tales from the harbour and the shadowy haunts of the city. *"The HMS Bengal case seems a lifetime away, doesn't it?"* murmured Arun, not looking up from his work. Blackthorn chuckled softly, *"Indeed, Constable. But let us not forget the thrill of that chase. There is always a rogue wave on calm seas."*

Their reflective moment was shattered by an urgent rapping at the door. "Come!" Blackthorn's voice was firm but not unkind. Sergeant Brady burst in, his florid face glistening with exertion. He paused, gasping for air, and then managed to convey the grim news. *"Inspector, they've found a woman... murdered, by the docks."* Blackthorn's brow furrowed with concern. *"Details, Sergeant. I trust there are more?"* Brady nodded, still struggling for breath. *"The constables believe she's... well, she's not from the dregs, sir. Looks to be a lady, well-bred and all."* Annoyance flickered across Blackthorn's features, but he masked it quickly. *"A lady, you say.*

Curious..." He snatched up his coat with a swift motion.

Arun, catching the shift in his mentor's demeanour, straightened. *"Back to the streets, then Inspector?"* *"Precisely,"* Blackthorn confirmed, striding to the door. *"Come Constable, we've a dark business to attend to."* The air outside was heavy with moisture as they made for the waiting handsome cab. As Blackthorn settled inside the conveyance, Arun saw the familiar fire igniting within the Inspector's eyes — the chase was afoot once more, and despite the grim circumstances, it was a welcome return to form. Arun could not help but feel the stirrings of excitement himself. "It's strange, Inspector," he confided as the cab lurched forward, *"but part of me has missed this — the pursuit, the unravelling of a new mystery."*

Blackthorn grinned, the grim reality of their profession doing little to stifle his zeal. "*Ah, Constable Verma, to be on the trail again, it's like a draught of strong ale after a long abstinence, is it not? Now, let's hasten to the scene and see what truths await us.*" With that, Blackthorn rapped sharply on the roof of the cab, urging the driver into a brisk trot. As the misty streets of London rolled by, the sensation of the impending inquiry eclipsed the somber mood of the day. They were back in their element, and London's shadowy underbelly had new secrets to reveal.

THE END

ABOUT THE AUTHOR

B R Bhanu

Delve into the narrative tapestry woven by B
R Bhanu, an emergent storyteller who has
transitioned from a career in commerce to
the venerable craft of writing. Bhanu's foray
into literature is marked by a dedication to
crafting narratives that captivate and
resonate deeply with his audience. He
possesses a unique talent for conjuring
stories from the obscure recesses of history and the chilling voids
of the human psyche.

Bhanu's literary creations transport readers into atmospheres
laden with suspense and shadow. His settings range from the
ghostly silhouettes of ancient manors and the luminescent
expanses of desolate heaths to the serpentine alleys of bygone eras
where whispers of secrets abound, and perils lurk at every turn.
His narratives are a homage to timeless folklore, cryptic enigmas,
and the limitless realms of his imagination, resulting in tales that
are as exquisitely crafted as they are thrilling.

The characters crafted by Bhanu are memorable and complex,
featuring detectives with a touch of old-world charm and villains
whose sinister plans are as deep and dark as the ocean's trenches.
These characters leap off the page, ensnaring readers in a
whirlwind of feelings, suspense, and intrigue.

But Bhanu's identity extends beyond his written words. He is a voracious seeker of hidden stories, reviving forgotten sagas with renewed vigour and contemporary flair. To Bhanu, every shadow tells a story, every dilapidated structure whisper secrets, and he is the medium through which these silent voices find expression in our world.

Printed in Great Britain
by Amazon

33552967R00066